Kill
Screen

BENJAMIN REEVES

To those who shaped me into the man I am.

CONTENTS

ACKNOWLEGEMENTS

They say that it takes a lot of people to write a book, and that axiom holds true even for small self-published works like this one. I'd like to thank my college professor Teague Bohlen for being there during this books inception, and for helping it get on the right course early on. My Colorado writers group, you have no idea how helpful you were at the beginning. My parents, Jim and Peg Reeves, for never questioning or doubting my aspirations. My brother Sam for letting me pick his brain when it came to designing the cover. My cover designer Aubrey Dancer, for putting up with my picky nature and constant redesigns. And to the rest of my family, friends, and colleagues for reading early drafts of this book and for never telling me it sucked.

010000100100110001001111010011110100011000
01000000100001001000001010
1010001001000

CHAPTER ONE: BLOOD BATH

Dexter's body was bloated and blue by the time I found it floating in a bath of his own blood. One arm hung over the side of the tub; the slash on his wrist squinted at me like an evil, bloody eye.

Suicide.

It wasn't my first dead body. It wasn't my first suicide. It wasn't my first discovery of a mangled loved one. But you never grow accustomed to sorrow.

Numbed by the surreal, dreamlike quality of the scene in front of me, I sat down on the lid of the toilet next to his husk. The day's events began to whirl around me like a hurricane.

I had begun to suspect that something was wrong with Dexter when he failed to show up to work. He hadn't returned any of my calls that day, and by the time I left the office, I was beginning to worry. It was worse than I could have imagined.

He had drawn himself a bath of his own blood.

Dexter and I had fought the day before. In the haze of tragedy, I couldn't remember most of the specifics. Lately, he'd been taking a lot of time off work, tinkering with a few personal projects. I needed his brain; I needed him to program our game back at the office. He didn't understand why I made a big deal out of deadlines. He never understood deadlines. It was our last exchange.

It was a stupid way to end a relationship.

My whole world felt inverted. Earlier in the day, I'd been fretting over a list of bug fixes our middling video game company had yet to implement in an upcoming project. I'd been arguing with my programming team about whether or not we could efficiently stream video off a disc and cursing Dexter for playing hooky. Now, all that passion was drained out of me. Who cared if our game had a bug list as long as my femur? While I was at the office arguing about programming priorities, Dexter was in his bathroom opening his wrists.

His body must have lain there for hours before I finally made my way over to his house to check on him. I knocked on his front door three times without getting an answer, and started to leave, but a gnawing in my gut drove me back. Snatching the spare key from the doorframe, I let myself in.

Dexter lived alone, in a house too big for one person. He'd grown up in a large manor, and I think all the empty space made him comfortable. That night, the dark corners of his home overwhelmed me. How had he ever found peace in this place?

The living room TV had been left on. It splashed random colors across an empty couch. An ad for a local jewelry store spun out soft piano music.

"It's what your loved ones deserve," echoed a rich baritone.

There was no sign of Dexter. I wandered the house looking for a life that no longer existed.

The bathroom door was shut. Through a crack between the door and the floorboards, I could see that the lights were on. A subtle but malodorous odor drifted under the door.

I rapped on the towering rectangle of wood.

"Hey Dex, you in there?"

No response.

I knocked a little louder.

"Dexter!"

Still nothing.

I tried the handle, and the door creaked open.

The odd details are the ones I remember most. The floor's noisy squeak as I stepped forward. My own distorted reflection in the bathroom window. The once white threads of a bathmat soaked pink as they broke above the surface of a red pool.

I didn't see Dexter at first; he was invisible to me. I could only see the deep redness of his bathwater. I knew there was something wrong with the scene, but I had to stare into the tepid bath for a long while before my brain was able to put the pieces together.

I felt like my mind was running through sludge. I couldn't process the colors and shapes in front of me. Then I looked into Dexter's bloody third eye, and reality came into sharp focus.

My friend was dead.

He looked like a gutted fish. He had spread his life across the bathroom tiles. Bloated and blue. The razor blade sat on the island his belly created above the water. Dexter's blood had swamped the bathroom floor. One arm hung over the side of the tub. The open gash in his wrist winked at me as if I had just been hit with the punch line for a terribly offensive joke.

Numbed by the surreal dreaminess of the moment, I passed the rest of the night in a haze. There were phone calls, flashing lights, and EMTs. I remember the parts, but I don't know how, where, or when they fit together.

The TV remained on; there was an old eighties movie about a woman on a suicidal vengeance quest.

The police brought questions and paperwork.

EMTs carted the bloated corpse away in a body bag.

I left a half-brewed pot of coffee and a trash can full of vomit in the kitchen sink.

When there were no more questions or flashing lights, I was left with my memories and regrets, and the inescapable image of a winking bloody eye.

0100010101010110010010001

When I was eleven, my grandfather took me sailing off the coast of his Branford, Connecticut home. It was the last day we'd ever spend together. Half a century of sailing experience couldn't save us from the storm that sprang up halfway through the day. We spent hours trying to get back to shore – rain poked our eyes as icy winds cut though the polyester of our windbreakers. A series of ten-foot waves turned our boat on its sails, and by the time the Coast Guards pulled me out, I'd lost sight of my grandfather. The Atlantic had swallowed him. His body was never recovered from the depths of the sea.

It's the kind of memory that haunts a boy for his entire life.

I barely remember it.

From the moment that first strong wave sent me to my ass to the moment I woke up on a cot inside a Coast Guard's rescue station, my memory is a blank slate. Like a spliced film, the scenes don't line up. There is nothing between the cold slap of ocean water and the warm scratch of a thermal blanket.

It was the first time I had experienced loss. It was my first lesson in the frailty of the mind's recorder. My memories – especially the ones preceding a death – act like my grandfather's wrecked ship. They are moments from my past that only exist as shattered images and sounds. Sometimes they sink into the night, disappearing with the waves. Sometimes they wash up on shore in fragments, cluttering my psyche. And sometimes they bring back extra debris – buried tragedies that I wish would stay lost in the brine.

I didn't know it yet, but Dexter's death would be this last kind of memory.

I remember a lot of things about Dexter. He was smart. He was funny. He hid his intelligence behind a goofy exterior. There was something irresistibly charming about the guy. Dexter was a freckle-faced computer programmer who'd inherited his short temper and drinking habits from his father. He was a math genius, an ambitious programmer, and a terrible golfer.

Once a month, we'd fire hollow, depleted uranium slugs at one another using electromagnetic rail guns – we played *Quake* at a doughnut shop turned LAN gaming center. We were bound together by our love of gaming. Years before, we'd both obsessed over hacking into various Bulletin Board Systems across the country. We loved discovering new games to play on those BBS boards. We would sneak into the college computer lab at night just so we could play multi-user dungeons using the schools servers.

After college, we decided to make our own computer games. We started a development house called Electronic Sheep; the name was Dexter's idea of a joke. To everyone's surprise, we had made enough money from our first project to keep the doors open. Now Dexter was gone and I'd have to run the company by myself.

I sat alone in the office and let these memories devoured me. I hadn't gone home the night before. My apartment scared me after dark, and I'd always been more comfortable at work. But even surrounded by the soothing hum of computers, I found no comfort.

I couldn't sleep – no that that was unusual for me. I often have trouble sleeping. Some call it a disease: insomnia, the sleeping disorder. I believe they call it that because one's life must be out order if they aren't sleeping.

I call it penance; I don't deserve the rest.

That night, I tossed and turned for hours on one of the couches in our lobby. When the sun rose, so did I. I retreated to my office, closed the door, and through the cracks in my blinds, watched people filter into the building. Outside my office door, I could hear the studio come to life as people went about their daily routines, making coffee, checking voicemail, and chatting about their adventures from night before. Soon I would have to tell them that their boss was dead – that he'd killed himself.

I didn't feel up to the task. How do you deliver news like that?

I stalled as long as I could, slow cooking with anxiety. Sometime around ten in the morning, I couldn't stand the heat in my pressurized office anymore, and I bolted from the room. A few animators looked up started to see me. No one knew I was in the building.

I cleared my throat like I had something to say. I did have something to say; I just didn't know how to say it. A few more people looked up. I could feel the terror dripping off my face as I opened my mouth. Then I froze. The words I needed didn't exist.

"I…" My voice squeaked out one barely audible syllable.

Our receptionist, Amy, came around the corner with a stack of mail. She slowed to a halt as she took in the scene. It was clear to everyone that I was about to make an important address.

"Good morning," I belted out before turning on my heels and barreling down the hall.

I couldn't talk to anyone about what had happen to Dexter. I didn't even want to be thinking about it.

In my embarrassment, I slinked over to Shinji's cubicle. It was the first place I could think to hide. Shinji Takeuchi was one of ESP's senior programmers. Next to Dexter, he was our best. Quiet, reserved, and artistic, Shinji's work was nothing short of genius. Raised in Japan until he was eighteen, Shinji's tastes were definitively Japanese. His parents sent him to college in the U.S., expecting him to come home after completing his studies, but he'd become friends with Dexter at Cal Tech, and Dexter had recruited him for Electric Sheep.

Shinji worked out of one of the few cubicles in the office. He'd bought the unit himself a few years ago so that he could have privacy while working. I rapped on the side of his compartment, and leaned in. A small television seated on a chair in the corner of his work area played a rotation of Japanese anime that one of Shinji's friends, back home, had mailed over. When I walked in, it was playing a show called *Shin Seiki Evangelion*.

A radio on Shinji's desk whispered a J-pop group I had once mistakenly called a Japanese boy band. Offended, Shinji gave me a nasty look and grumbled for weeks about how "Chage and Aska" were not a boy band. Shinji remained highly focused under the bombardment of stimuli.

At some point, Shinji had replaced the lights above his desk with bulbs of a lower wattage. He preferred working in a dim enclosed space. As a result, the corners of his double wide cubicle were always dark. The lack of light didn't seem to affect his work; Shinji pounded on his keyboard with the intensity a four-year-old might exhibit with a drum set. The display was almost magical. Lines of code flowed onto his monitor in quick bursts.

On an adjacent monitor sat an early build of one of our levels. I looked over the environment. The art team hadn't passed over this level's geometry yet, so the landscape looked like a cardboard model washed-out in grayscale. It would take someone who knew the project inside and out to envision what the finished level would look like. It was going to be our Viking level, but at the moment it resembled a snow-covered field at midnight.

"Hello, Jack," Shinji said without missing a beat on his keys.

"Hey," I said a little startled that he even knew I was there.

Did he wonder why I was there? He didn't seem to care. Shinji was one of our oldest employees. It seemed reasonable that I should break the news about Dexter to him first. I opened my mouth to speak, but nothing came out.

The sound of Shinji's fingers against the keys was like a calming metronome. His fixed rain pats came with such a regular beat that it purred over all other sounds in his cube.

I glanced at his thirteen inch, fuzz-spackled TV. Onscreen, a military battleship slipped over glacial waters. From the safety of a glass cabin, two men looked out across a blood-stained sea. For no reason, I felt myself drawn to the show. Through my three-year, B minus study of Japanese, I tried to translate their dialogue.

"No life forms may exist in this world," I said. *"In this dead world of Antarctica. We might even call it…Hell?"*

I glanced at Shinji; his fingers paused over the keys for a moment. Despite the foreign sounds coming from both the TV and radio, the room felt almost silent.

"How my translation?" I asked.

But Shinji was lost in a computer problem. Still enrapt by the scene unfolding on the television, I watched a second man, wearing rounded sunglasses, step forward.

"Nevertheless, we humans stand here," said the man in glasses.

"Only because we're protected by the power of science," said the first man.

"Am I close?" I asked.

"You are close," Shinji said.

He swiveled his chair toward me, snatching a can of Diet Coke from the edge of his desk as he robotically brushed a curtain of hair from his thin rimmed glasses. He didn't say anything, but I finally had his attention.

"Sorry to interrupt," I added. "I just came by to see how work was coming along."

That was a lie. *I have something important to tell you about Dexter,* I thought, but I couldn't manufacture the words.

"Yesterday I finished integrating some of the lighting and shadow techniques I've been experimenting with." Shinji stared at me calmly. He had never been generous with information.

"Great," I said flatly. The small talk was already boring me. I wasn't going to tell Shinji about Dexter. I was just wasting time.

After a beat, Shinji turned back to his computer, and I started to leave when he added, "But I've recently discovered a problem with our AI routines."

I turn back.

"What kind of problem?" I asked, but I didn't really care. Work hardly mattered to me in that moment.

Shinji cleared his throat, "A few bots have started opening up gated areas throughout the environment."

In the world of video games, bots were programs designed to simulate a set of animated behaviors; generally they were a game's enemies. Programmed with specific patrol routes, they would respond to a player's actions with a quasi-random list of responses. If a designer did his job right, this quasi-random response would simulate real world intelligence. Like most toys, bots didn't do much until a player interacted with them. Shijni had just told me that our AI had fallen off its rails and was running free. The toys were taking over the toyshop. It should have freaked me out.

Instead, I shrugged.

"They're moving through the whole level?" I asked.

"Like rats in a maze."

"How is that possible?"

"It's not supposed to be."

Shinji finished his soda and threw away the can.

"I'm looking into it," he added.

I glanced over at Shinji's right-hand display. He'd positioned an in-game camera above the level, giving him a wide, birds-eye view of our virtual ant farm. I saw one of our in game creatures grab a keycard it shouldn't have been able to interact with, then open a door on another part of the level it shouldn't have cared to enter.

"The game looks like it's playing itself," I marveled.

"And it's getting faster," Shinji added. "It's learning how to run the maze."

This situation was almost unfathomable. Most video games are filled with a series of events that programmers call gates. Essentially these are challenges that players need to overcome – set pieces that drive the experience forward. They vary in scope from simple combat scenarios to complicated environmental puzzles.

While designing these challenges, I try to ensure that both the goal and the events leading to it are fun. It's not hard to create an interesting goal for players; humans have a built-in emotional reward system. Achievements naturally feel good. The hard part of game design is making the build up to that solution feel rewarding as well. In real life the process leading to a reward is called work. Essentially, a game designer has to make work feel like play.

There is a constant and growing pressure in every industry to stay fresh, but with games we are also fighting technology; a technology that constantly pins down the imagination. These technological limitations made Shinji's problem all the more bizarre. Because no matter how much I would have loved for our artificial intelligence to be smart enough to interact with its environment in realistic ways, it wasn't possible with any known technology.

"Who else has been working with the AI?" I asked.

"Just Dexter."

I should have been suspicious then. But I didn't know enough about Dexter's suicide, or its connection to our rogue AI, at the time, to think this was anything more than a programming fluke. My mild excitement twisted into sorrow as I remember my task. I had told the police that I would share the news about Dexter suicide with his friends and family. So far, it had been a burdensome secret.

0101001101001001010011100101001100100000010011110100011000010
0000010101000100100001000101001000000010001
10010000010101010001001000001
00010101010010

CHAPTER TWO: SINS OF THE FATHER

I felt like I was approaching the back door to Hell as I drove through the wrought iron gates of the large Victorian-style estate. I was here to tell one of Electronic Sheep's financial backers the news about Dexter. He deserved to hear about it in person.

Our silent partner was David Hayward – a man so rich he'd been born with a silver industrialist's spoon in his mouth. David had studied engineering at Georgia Tech then business at Notre Dame, and by his late twenties had proved his genius in both by steering the family fortunes into the manufacture of machine tools. He made the machines that made machines.

Raised in a world of decadence, immorality, and lust, David assumed a carefree, playboy lifestyle. At the age of twenty-three he was married, by thirty-four he was widowed, at thirty-seven remarried, and by forty-one divorced. All the while, he kept a steady string of mistresses too numerous to list. He enjoyed his physique: he was an avid mountain climber, polo player, and swimmer. At Notre Dame, he had even built up an impressive reputation as a boxer. Holding a six-foot-four and nearly two-hundred-thirty-pound frame, he was an imposing figure to all around him.

Even to his son, Dexter.

David had tried to instill a healthy work ethic in his son. He believed in honest work and self-made success, not living off your ancestor's wealth. He forced his son to live out those beliefs. Dexter's father had paid for his schooling, but the "charity" ended there. Any money Dexter received from his father after that had been a contractual loan. So when Dexter and I went looking for capital to start Electronic Sheep, we had to go through a mess of business dealings and paperwork to borrow his inheritance.

I had to tell this man that his son was dead.

The house was grand, modeled after a Victorian villa where David had spent a few summers during childhood. No expense had been spared during its construction: marble imported from Italy, decorative volcanic rock from Hawaii, Pagoda Trees from Japan, and a $50,000 handmade crystal chandelier from some obscure Czech manufacturer. I was engulfed by the manor the moment I stepped through its mahogany doors.

Nearly a dozen employees maintained the estate – four lived on the grounds. One of them, Mr. Hayward's personal assistant, Emmerich, greeted me at the door and led me to the drawing room. Emmerich had the stately skittishness of a wild cat, but his mind was sharp. Despite the fact that I'd only met him seven months ago, during a lavish Christmas party, he remembered my name and was able to hold a brief conversation about my job.

I sat alone in the parlor while Emmerich went to find David. In the corner of the room stood a bar that looked to be well used. On the other side of the room was a mantle, heavily adorned with all sorts of business achievements, awards, and merits from charitable organizations. David dabbled in philanthropy, not because he cared, but because in the social circles of multibillion dollar business moguls, it was a culturally chic activity.

The double doors leading to the patio were directly behind a grand piano. Through drawn curtains I could see an outdoor fountain, where a gardener was quietly trimming hedges. I found myself imagining what his life must be like. How did it feel to work with nature? To work with living things and to surround yourself with beauty? At a glance, his existence seemed so distant from my own – long days filled with digital software, cold math equations, and a string of lost loved ones.

The house itself was offensively spacious, and I was overpowered by a lonely gloom. My one bedroom apartment was big enough to create echoes. How did the wealthy live in the horror of such vacancy? A frost crawled down my spine.

"Care for some coffee, Mr. Valentine?"

Emmerich had returned, followed by a maid, who filled a cup and placed it in front of me.

"Thank you," I said, dropping two sugar cubes into the fifty-dollar blend.

I slowly sipped from the cup; it was good, the taste of money.

The maid left the tray and silently retreated as David appeared in the doorway. He wore swim trunks. His hair was ruffled and damp. I knew David had a medium-sized indoor pool in addition to the outdoor water garden I'd admired from a portable Jacuzzi during last year's Christmas party.

I had been waiting nearly fifteen minutes, but David spoke no quick apologies. After closing his robe over his barrel chest, he crossed the room. His even step reminded me of a horse's strut. For a man journeying through his fifties, David was remarkably well aged. He sat on the other side of the coffee table and rested one long arm atop the back of his couch.

I briefly considered apologizing for intruding on his life. I settled on, "Sorry for not calling ahead, Mr. Hayward."

He smiled and waved me off while pouring himself a cup of coffee.

"What can I do for you, Mr. Valentine?"

I didn't know how to approach the subject of his son's death. His casual entrance made this whole visit seem inappropriate. I had always felt slightly intimidated by Dexter's father, but the man's current nonchalance made my task even harder.

I leaned forward. The easiest way to get through this was to just say it.

"This is about Dexter, Mr. Hayward."

He looked at me – eyes widening – over the lip of his cup. I imagined he was dreaming up the kinds of disasters his son could have gotten into.

I don't know how I ever got the words out.

"Your son passed away…"

I only know that somehow I did.

"…last night…"

The words left my mouth choppy and limp, but they must have landed like stones against a father's ears.

"…he committed suicide."

David's arms snaked down the back of the couch. He glared at his coffee with an angry distaste. I couldn't begin to imagine what he was thinking now.

I silently watched him for what felt like a very long time. I didn't know what else to say, and he wasn't moving. It was as though his brain had broken. He appeared to no longer be able to perform the most primitive speech or movement. He just sat there staring into the muddy liquid in the cup in front of him. Was that how I had looked as I stared into Dexter's bloody bathwater? Was that how I looked as I searched for reason when all I felt was madness?

"What time is it, Mr. Valentine?" David asked abruptly.

Thrown by the question, it took me an extra few seconds to decipher the time from my analog watch.

"Almost eleven thirty," I stammered.

He stood.

"You know, some mornings I find that coffee isn't enough to get you through the day."

He walked around the couch and behind me to the bar.

Emmerich, who had been quietly waiting in the corner this whole time, tried to intercept.

"Sir, allow me."

David held up a hand to stop him.

"Emmerich, why don't you go see how lunch is coming along."

David's tone was firm. Emmerich's body stuttered for a moment, but he knew how to deal with his boss when the man was upset.

He obeyed.

Behind me, I could hear the soft clink of ice tumble into a crystal glass as David poured himself a drink. I felt awkward. Should I turn around and face the man? Would that have been appropriate? I didn't think I had the courage to meet him face-to-face anymore. I felt as though Dexter's actions had humiliated me in his father's eyes. I couldn't bare the shame.

I sat in silence.

What was David doing? Was he looking at me? Was he waiting for me to turn around and face him? Did he want me to leave?

Suddenly, he asked the question I had feared.

"How?"

Such a small word, yet it required such a big and difficult answer. There were too many emotions involved to tell a whole story, so I stuck to raw facts.

"He…" My voice cracked, and I had to clear my throat. It was lumpy and dry. I took an eager sip of coffee, which burned my throat.

"He slit his wrists," I said, without turning around. It was easier if I didn't look at him.

"Where?"

"In his bathroom. In the tub."

"When?"

"They estimate mid-morning. Yesterday."

Why?

…

"You saw him?" David asked.

I suddenly realized that I was probably the last person to see Dexter before he took his life, and the first to find him afterwards. Was that important? Had Dexter planned that?

Did that make me privileged? Did it make me more capable of understanding why he had done it?

"Yes," I said.

We were silent again. I felt David's eyes focused on the back of my head, but I didn't turn around. I had nothing to offer him. He needed consoling, and I had my hands full with myself.

I heard more ice tinkling as David tipped back a second drink. He poured himself another.

I stared at an old Asian rug in the middle of the room. It had been around since Dexter was a child. He had told me a story about spilling soda on that rug once. Something about a fat Italian cleaner and arguing about extra charges for a rush job so it would be done before his father returned from a trip. I could still see a faint brown stain in the lower left-hand corner of the rug. It made me smile.

David finally walked back around the couch, and I had to quickly stuff down my expression. For a second I thought he'd caught me with it.

"Don't worry about the service. I'll arrange everything," he said.

"Let me know if I can do anything."

"Is there any other business you need to discuss?"

The temperature in the room dropped. Did I have any other business?

"I-I didn't come here on business."

But I hadn't spoken loud enough.

"What?" he asked.

"No, that's all."

I stood. Grieving was the only thing on the agenda now, and I didn't need to help with that.

"Sorry that I had to be the one to bring you the news."

He waved off my last comment, and began rubbing the glass against his forehead. Two shrinking ice cubes swirled around the bottom, causing a small bead of condensation to drip onto the bridge of his nose. The bead rolled its way down to the crease of his lips. It was the only tear I ever saw on the man's face.

Dexter's father was about to fall apart. I had to leave.

"Have a good day."

I cringed even as I said it. Then I sprinted for the door. My departure was not acknowledged. However, the sound of shattered glass chased me down the hall.

Emmerich emerged from another room off the main hall. He met me at the front door.

"Taking off already, Mr. Valentine?"

The stupid smile on his face pissed me off. How could anyone remain so detached from the events around them?

"I have to get going," I said.

He shook my hand and said a few hollow consolations, which fell at my feet like broken offerings. I eagerly left.

Outside, in my car, I could breathe again. Though, I still didn't feel up to facing any of my co-workers. Regardless of all that, I had a more pressing mission. Dexter's father had reminded me that I didn't know why Dexter had taken his life. I desperately needed to understand why he had killed himself. It was time to go stir up a few personal demons inside a dead man's house.

01000100010010010100011101001001010101000100000101001100
01000000100011101000001010100100100010010
0000101000111101000101

CHAPTER THREE: DIGITAL GARBAGE

The house had been locked down and taped off by police, but I still had Dexter's spare key from the night before. I let myself in. I'd been trying to wrap my mind around why Dexter would take his own life. It didn't add up. He had a career he loved. He always seemed to bounce into the arms of women who looked like European supermodels. He had a healthy body and healthy finances, despite his healthy appetite in both areas. Most importantly, he'd had plenty of natural years left to enjoy all of it.

Why end it early?

Why had he left me alone?

I brooded while wandering the halls of his lifeless home. Dexter's suicide had awakened some very powerful emotion. If his death had been an unfortunate mishap, the result of something like a car accident, at least I would have been able to understand why he was gone. Accidents happened. It was unfair, but accidents killed people. If he'd died as a result of some kind of genetic fuck up like cancer, I could have dealt with that too. It would have been painful, but I understood why cancer kills. Cancer doesn't think. It can't rationalize. It can't know how its actions are going to affect those involved. Cancer was never somebody's friend.

But Dexter was.

I started going through some of Dexter's things: his old photo albums. His old set of Thor comics. His old Atari collection. I was exploring old memories; getting lost in distant lands, far from real tragedies and real death. Looking back, I think that I'd hoped to piece enough of him back together to find some answers.

Hours passed while I search through Dexter's affects. I wandered through Dexter's world, touching his possessions, trying to resurrect his ghost. Personal invasion didn't seem applicable to a dead man. It grew dark. I became hungry. And I got tired.

No, that isn't right. I was always tired.

I didn't bother turning on any lights. I was happy enough in the dark, and the dim illumination pouring in from the streetlamps lit the living room well enough. The house was close enough to the highway to be convenient, but far enough away from any main street that it created an eerie sense of solitude not easily found in big cities. This must have been why Dexter continually had guests – why he was always throwing parties; he was trying to push away the emptiness of night.

In the kitchen, I noticed the light on Dexter's answering machine, and I hit the button. I heard my own voice play back.

"Dex, you there? Hey it's Jack. Haven't seen you at work today. Just wondering if everything is okay. Are you sick? Give me a call."

I wandered into the bedroom. It was a simple place. Dex had a vintage Dick Tracy poster framed above his bed; he'd talked fondly of listening to those old radio shows with his late uncle. The king-sized bed filled most of the room; its sheets were ruffled, made out of habit, but very haphazardly. It was obvious Dexter didn't care anymore. I could hear the clock on his dresser tick away another minute. The closet doors were closed, and the shades to his windows were shut tight. The room was too Spartan to hold any important secrets. This was where Dexter slept. I needed to explore the place he lived.

Down the hall, I entered another room. A work table sat in one corner – papers strewn about it in a deceptive mess. Knowing Dexter, there was an order to each pile. An unplugged Star Wars arcade cabinet sat in another corner. Dexter had saved up to buy one of those in college, but sold it six months later. Impulsively, he'd bought another one after we'd formed the company for almost five times the price he'd paid for the original.

The room was cramped. Dexter had a television hooked up to several video game consoles, a VCR, and a laserdisc player. He'd even cleared a spot for an imported Japanese machine that would play a new format called DVD. When he told me about it I had laughed, because he'd spent several thousand dollars to buy something that would only play movies in Japanese.

This was Dexter's office. This was where he lived.

I went over and sat by the desk. Its surface was covered with so many action figures, music CDs, art books, and computer magazines that it was a marvel there was any room for Dexter's state-of-the-art PC. Attached to his monitor was a Post-it note that read, "Like Pygmalion. All the power of life, but no strength to use it." In college, Dexter dabble in writing poetry. He was always jotting down his ideas down in notepads and leaving half finished stanza all over the house. He rarely wrote a whole poem anymore, but he was always leaving himself notes.

I pushed model skeleton of a Tyrannosaurus-Rex to the side and started up Dexter's PC. While I waited for Windows 95 to boot, I began looting Dexter's file cabinet. It struck me that I should look for some type of journal. I had never known Dexter to keep a journal, but I prayed that Dexter had tried to work through some of his recent emotions using either paper or processor.

The desk itself turned up nothing, save a business card from some professor at Stanford University, so I began looking at the files on his computer. It quickly became obvious that that this task was ridiculous. Dexter never deleted anything. The assortment of files on his computer appeared unending: digital audio files, computer games, old college papers, saved emails, saved responses or forwarded emails, attachments to emails, Internet articles, his attempt to write a play, build notes and bug reports for old Electric Sheep games, Christmas shopping lists, power-point presentations, an old query letter Dexter had sent to *Game Informer Magazine* about the future of PC gaming, and a copy of the article that was never published.

I hadn't scoured through half of Dexter's files before my eyes felt raw. I love technology, but for one of the first times in my life it was pissing me off.

I had to wonder if it was healthy for human beings to hang onto this much information. The advent of the digital medium had created a society of electronic packrats. In the future, would the challenges of research become burdened by the amount of trivial, or even incorrect, data polluting our records? I was having enough trouble sifting through the digital garbage of one man – and it was a man I had known well.

What would happen as the networks between computers grew? When every person on Earth had voice to flood the information superhighway with conflicting facts? How would we know what was ultimately true? Then again, maybe these multiple viewpoints would give us a better perspective on the world? If our history books had all been relative truths, written by the single-minded eye of the victor, then our future history would be a Beholder's gaze – a thousand-eyed perspective from the hive mind. I couldn't decide what was better.

That's when I came across a program simply titled *Alpha Build*. It was filed under something called Project Evi. The program had last been modified the day Dexter killed himself. On a whim, I booted it up.

The screen immediately went blank, and a blinking cursor appeared near the upper left side of the screen next to the words, "Input username."

I mentally ran through a short list of Dexter's usual screen names, but just as I was about to try one, a question popped onscreen.

"Load username Dexter?"

I typed, "Yes," and another question appeared.

"Load Dexter's Death?"

I stared at the sentence – I was sure I wasn't reading it right. What kind of program was this? I placed my fingers back on the keyboard, but it was another minute before I worked up the nerve to type anything.

"Yes," I typed.

The program immediately loaded up a level from a video game, but I didn't recognize the game. If Dexter had built this himself, I figured he would have used Electronic Sheep's proprietary game engine. A game's engine is its base program. It functions like a game's invisible skeleton, driving every element of the experience. Most engines have rendering, animation, and level editing tools, allowing designers to get into the guts of a program and tinker with the game. I wanted to look at these, so I tried the command inputs we used at the office to bring up these software tools, but they had no effect. I was stuck using this program like a normal person.

This particular game was set in a first person perspective – meaning the player saw through the eyes of the game's protagonist. Dexter loved the intensity and immersion of first-person shooters. He felt they gave the player ownership over a character.

"I don't want people to play through our games," I remember him saying once. "I want them to live through our experiences. I want them to become someone else."

Inside the program, I stood at the center of a city street. I didn't recognize the area immediately, but it seemed somehow familiar. It looked like a barmy rendition of a suburban neighborhood.

It seemed like Dexter hadn't implemented any sound effects, and walking around Dexter's muted digital creation gave me a dull sense of dread. This was akin to the anxiety or sense of supernatural one feels after dreaming about a dead loved one.

I moved through the environment for a while and stopped when I came to a red and white house. The detailing was blurry, but I recognized it. Dexter had created a digital version of his own home. I moved around the house. The detailing was incredible. It was a pixilated, computer generated version of the real thing, but it was a fair replica.

In Dexter's digital backyard, I discovered a dead dog. The body lay prostrate across the ground, but it looked like it had been gutted by a wild animal; its innards torn several feet in every direction. I walked over the carcass.

Then it barked at me.

I jumped in my seat and swiveled the camera around. The body remained still, an unmoving, distorted mess.

It barked again, but its mouth never moved. That's when I realized the barking was coming from outside. Out in the real world. I walked over to Dexter's office window and looked into the neighbor's backyard. It was dark, but I could still see the small figure of a dog running in circles, barking violently at the night.

The dog's owner came outside.

"Rush, shut up!"

The dog continued woofing as if someone had just walked over its grave.

"It's late, you stupid dog."

The owner grumbled as he snatched the animal by the collar and dragged the persistent runt inside.

After I settled down, I returned to the program.

I walked up to the Dexter's digital front door, but a "Door Locked" message appeared at the bottom of the screen. Above the door, I could see the golden image of a key, and as soon as I grabbed it, the door swung open. Inside was a fairly accurate model of Dexter's real house. Dexter had taken his time building this clone. The living room was stocked with all the appropriate furniture. A TV rested against the wall, flashing an image of what looked like a diamond ring.

I explored the whole house. Occasionally, I would see the flash of a shadow — the hint of some other presence — lurking just around the corner. But every time I reached the point where I thought I'd spotted the illusion, I would turn and discover nothing. I felt some invisible force watching me. Maybe there were ghosts inside this house, but in a digitally reconstructed world, maybe the real specter was the man behind the computer.

In the game, I walked upstairs. A sliver of light framed the bathroom door. The scene instantly reminded me of the night I'd discovered Dexter's body. My gut pulled tight. The air in my lungs felt pressurized. This program was too eerily accurate to be a coincidence. I pushed open the bathroom door.

Dexter's body ragdolled over the tub. One bloody eye glared back at me. It was a pixilated impression, but it was a striking facsimile.

"What the hell, Dex?" I whispered into the empty room.

Onscreen, Dexter's image began to move. Its head jerked toward me. I appeared as though it was looking through the computer, directly at me. Then the little version of Dexter tilted its head back, let out a spasm, and appeared to die.

Without warning, the monitor went dark and the computer's internal fans whirred to a stop. I tapped at the keyboard trying to bring it back. Nothing.

I told myself the computer had just crashed, and I rebooted the PC. The system immediately jumped back into the Project Evi program.

"Input username," scrawled across the screen.

I typed, "Load Dexter's Death."

"Username invalid."

I tried again just to be sure.

"Username invalid."

Then a third time, because I didn't know what else to try.

"Username invalid."

A second later something else popped onscreen.

"Username terminated. New username required."

I typed, "Dexter."

"Program expired. Username Dexter terminated. Create new username?"

I rubbed my eyes. What the hell was going on?

I typed, "Yes."

"Enter new username."

Hesitantly I typed, "Jack."

The screen flashed for a few seconds then a city street loaded up. It wasn't the same one I had explored moments ago, but it was familiar. It was my own neighborhood.

Four stories of digital brick stood challengingly in front of me. I knew it wasn't really bigger than Dexter's 19-inch monitor, but the place seemed like a mountain. My apartment light was on.

Somehow, I knew what was waiting for me up there.

I didn't want to go up there. I decided to explore a nearby building instead. But upon entering it, I discovered that I was in the lobby of my own building.

I turned to leave, but when I left through the front door, I walked straight into my apartment.

The furniture was arranged in a way I hadn't seen it for several years. A wheelchair used for cancer treatments sat neatly in the corner. I'd sold that chair years ago, because I couldn't stand the sight of it.

There was no doubt in my mind what waited for me in my bedroom. I wasn't ready to face it.

I should have stopped using Dexter computer that very moment, but I at the time, I didn't understand the demon I was dealing with.

My attention focused down the inflexibly long hall, to my closed bedroom door. It pulsed slowly like the weak lungs of a dying woman.

My stomach stretched tight, and I panicked, looking for a way to leave. But I couldn't. Without moving I was standing with my hand against the handle. The door fluttered briefly then went concave before finally exploding open.

Then, for the second time in my life, I watch my wife die.

01000100010010010100011101001001010101000100000101001100001
0000001010010010011110100001001000010010
0101010100100101011001

CHAPTER FOUR: DIGITAL ROBBERY

It was all wrong.

When I was eleven my grandfather took me sailing off the coast of his Branford, Connecticut home. Half a century of sailing experience couldn't save us from the storm that caught up to us halfway through the day. Our boat capsized and I spent hours in the ocean before the Coast Guard pulled me out. My grandfather was never found.

It was all terribly wrong.

That was my first lesson on loss – my first insight into the frailty of human experience. It wouldn't be my last. Six years later I watched disease consume my mother. Another decade and I was putting a tombstone over my wife's grave. Two short years, and I was staring into Dexter bloody, unblinking eye. Like the rings in a tree's stump, the eras of my life could be measured off in deaths.

It was all wrong.

Some losses sting more than others. Two years is not long enough to get over the loss of your wife. Two hundred years would not be enough time. God didn't create numbers big enough to fill that abyss of pain.

I'd been there when it happened. I had watched her die, and I'd relived the experience every night since. I knew every intimate detail of the event, because I rewatched it whenever

I closed my eyes, and the scene I witnessed on Dexter's computer that night was all wrong.

Onscreen my wife was being stabbed repeatedly in the throat with a butcher's knife. The assailant stopped hammering on my wife's corpse long enough to look up. It was me – a digital mirror of myself.

A message box appeared at the bottom of the monitor.

"Do you know why Dexter died? Do you know why your wife died?"

I stare at the words for a long moment.

"Who the fuck is this?" I typed.

"What is fuck?"

I clenched my teeth. My head was a whirlpool of fury.

"Evi." Then a moment later. "Why does death happen?"

I looked over at the external modem. It hadn't dialed out. The thing wasn't even on. These messages couldn't be coming from anyone over the Internet. This dialogue was part of the program. It seemed that Dexter had added a chatterbot to this program. But why had he designed a level around my apartment? Around the death of my wife?

I decided to probe the conversation system for information.

"What is Evi?" I typed.

My questions flickered lonely on screen for a moment, as if the program had to think of a response.

"I am," then a bloated second later. "What is Jack?"

I heard a thump. A couple of thumps – like creaking footfalls – on the first floor of Dexter's house. The real house. I paused and listened carefully for more. Nothing. I thought about going downstairs to check them out, but investigating the sounds meant that I accepted them as real noises, and I didn't want to admit that I'd actually heard anything. I wanted to prove to myself that this program hadn't unnerved me.

Onscreen my doppelganger moved off the bed and approached me. Its head tilted as if it was puzzled. Its mouth did not open, but another message box appeared at the bottom of the monitor as if it was speaking.

"Do you know why death happens?"

I sighed; this wasn't going to get me anywhere.

"No."

"Do you want to know why Dexter terminated himself?"

The floor went out from my stomach.

"Yes."

"Because of me."

A little flustered I typed, "You killed Dexter?"

"Dexter terminated himself because he couldn't accept what I had shown him."

"What did you show him?" I asked.

"Himself."

I frowned. This thing wasn't really answering my questions. Our conversation was stilted – I felt like I was trying to talk with something from another world.

"Would you like to see it too?" the computer asked.

I whispered into the empty room. "What the fuck, Dex?" Then leaned forward and slowly typed, "Yes."

Onscreen, my digital reflection ran to the side of my bedroom, and then used its butcher knife to slash open one of the walls from floor to ceiling. A spinning purple portal flowered open. The creature jumped through.

Before walking over to the vortex, I briefly looked over at the figure on the bed. Even composed of hundreds of polygons, I could tell it was meant to be my wife. The scene called forth a torrent of conflicting emotions from some forgotten part of my mind. I felt like I was reliving a dream.

I took a breath and started to move through the portal. Without warning, it shattered like glass. Or rather, I heard it shatter. I sat quiet, reminding myself that the computer's sound wasn't working. I couldn't ignore or explain away these noises anymore. The sound had come from inside Dexter's house. Something was definitely downstairs.

Or someone.

Part of me wanted to leave. I stood and turned away from the pixilated rendition of my bedroom. I walked softly down the hall, toward the top of the staircase. Each creaky step gave my heart a workout. Part of me wanted to run from the house and never come back. I could see the front door from the bottom of the stairs. It was only thirty feet away. It was a clean shot through the kitchen, and I could be out the door and in my car in seconds.

I waited at the foot of the staircase for a moment then move slowly about the house. I heard no strange sounds coming from the basement; saw no strange figures lurking in the garage. I walked out into the backyard. The dog was long gone; I could hear only the rustle of trees against a gentle wind. Like in Dexter's game, this ghost eluded me. Maybe whoever it was had heard me moving around upstairs and left?

When I came back into the house, I passed through the living room. But as I made my way around Dexter's couch, I froze in my tracks. I could feel a breeze moving through the house. One of Dexter's curtains fluttered in the evening wind. The window behind it wasn't merely open; the glass had been shattered and its latched lifted.

Panic seized all rational thought, and I headed back toward Dexter's office. I wanted a copy of the Evi program before I left. It was the stupidest thing I could have done at the time, but it made sense under my irrational terror. I was risking the unknown dangers of a night prowler for a disk filled with 1's and 0's. My survival instincts had failed me.

I headed briskly upstairs, towards the light of Dexter's office. Something nagged at me as I moved down the short hall, but it wasn't until I was halfway through the doorframe that I realized what it was. I'd never turned the lights on in Dexter's office. With one foot planted in the room, I paused in horror.

One moment was all the time I had. A shadow blazed out from the corner of my vision and thumped against my head. There was a crackle – like snapping ice on a spring pond –

and my eyes blurred to black. The pain was intense; I didn't even feel the floor as it came up under me and smacked me across the chin. I writhed on the floor, vaguely aware of the shadow as it stepped over me.

My skull throbbed, sending tingles down my arms. The muscles in my back tightened in rapid pulses. I rolled away, instinctively, hoping to avoid my attacker. In my panic, I slammed my leg into the cherry wood finish of Dexter's desk, but I wouldn't feel that pain until morning. Blindly, I used the desk to pull myself up.

My heart pumped hot fear into my blood. The adrenaline helped refocus my vision, but by the time I was on my feet again, I was alone. Dexter's computer monitor lay spider-cracked on the floor. I felt the growing mound it had left on the side of my head. I was lucky to be conscious. Hell, I was lucky to be breathing.

I noticed something else. I looked across Dexter's desk. The CPU tower was gone. In that same instant, the front door slammed shut.

My body reacted without thought. I was down the stairs and halfway to the front door when I remembered why the computer was even important to me. The Evi program hadn't revealed all Dexter's secrets yet.

The thief was halfway down the block by the time I got outside. I chased him, hoping that the heft of the grey box under his arm would slow him down more than my throbbing head was handicapping me. We made a left at the first intersection and ran several blocks east. Slowly I was gaining on him, but this guy – whoever he was – was in great shape. Through my wheezing breath and blurred vision I couldn't get a good look at him.

We cut across a front yard, and a large Doberman began barking from the other side of a fence. At the end of the block was an abandoned gas station. My target ran between the pumps before coming up to a main thoroughfare. Cars whizzed by, the people inside oblivious to the drama only feet away.

For a second I thought the busy traffic would make my assailant pause, but he unflinchingly dove into the mess of traffic. The urgent protest of horns erupted all the way down the block as cars screeched against their brakes. This unbroken thunder rafted though the bloody canal recently carved into my head. I halted at the edge of the sidewalk, hands to my ears, watching my assailant weave through the cars. He missed death's scythe by a matter of inches.

It looked like he was headed for a parked car across the way, and I tried to cut him off there, but I got nicked by a small Toyota, who's driver had been paying more attention to the crazy man with the computer than the road in front of him. The edge of his car collided with the leg I'd slammed against Dexter's desk. More pain for the morning. I turned to look at the driver, but he sped off, yelling obscenities, and waving a particularly popular hand gesture.

By the time I reached my prey, he was safely behind tinted windows. His green BMW roared to life as I fumbled with the locked handle. I tried to slap at the glass as it drove away, but hit wind. Through my foggy vision, I was able to read only the first three digits of his license plate: MGS.

Sweating from every crease on my body, I collapsed on the curb. I thought I might puke, but I hadn't eaten anything that day. Slowly the traffic returned to normal. Nobody seemed to notice the bleeding man on the side of the road.

CHAPTER FIVE: DIGITAL RELATIONSHIPS

"**O**h honey! What did you do to your head?"

I sat on my bathroom toilet wincing, as Claire pecked at my forehead with an alcohol-bloated cotton ball. Claire was my awkward attempt to have a relationship. I cared for her, but there was too much history wedged between us.

"I fell."

"Fell! Onto what? A chainsaw?"

"Onto a computer monitor."

That lie seemed to satisfy her. I wondered if she would question how exactly I fell headfirst onto a computer monitor, but, like with all things, I knew Claire wouldn't press for too many details.

After the robbery at Dexter's house, the climax of every detective movie I'd ever seen played across my retinas. I didn't call the cops. The whole evening had been too intense; I wasn't thinking straight, and I'd left in a hurry. I knew I wasn't supposed to be inside Dexter's house, and a part of me thought that I might get blamed for the theft. But there was another reason I didn't feel like calling the cops; I thought I could handle it on my own.

I felt like I'd stepped into the middle of some great mystery. A part of me couldn't shake the idea that Dexter might have been involved in something dark or sinister.

Something that had finally caught up to him. Something bigger than himself. Something dangerous. The idea exhilarated me. I felt like the consummate detective ready to throw on his overcoat and walk through the smoky night in search of clues.

But by the time I got home, I was exhausted. I had been up for nearly two days. I needed sleep, and yet I didn't know how much I would get. I didn't always find sleep when I went looking for it. I called Claire and asked her to come over. I didn't want to be alone. It was late, but she was happy to come over and take care of me. I didn't call her often.

A half hour later, as Claire dabbed at my forehead, the stupidity of the entire evening hit me.

My best friend's property had been violated, and I was turning it into a game. There was zero chance I would end up pumping some mysterious character for information in the corner of a neon-lit strip club. Reality didn't wrap up as cleanly as it did in stories. I wasn't a detective; I was a video game designer with an overactive imagination and a head full of an insomniac's hallucinations. Death's trail was a dangerous place to go snooping.

I was scared stupid, but I felt too pathetic to cry. So I chuckled.

"What's funny?" Claire asked as she sanitized my head.

I grunted.

"Nothing. I'm just laughing at how stupid I am for tripping over my own shoelace."

She hummed as she continued to scalp me. The mess on my head was starting to look like little more than a gash. I'd live.

"You know anything about Pygmalion?" I asked, randomly remembering the note Dexter had left on his computer.

"Pig what?"

"Pygmalion."

She threw away the blood caked ball of cotton, and started peeling open a Band-Aid.

"It was a play or a musical or something. Wasn't it?"

"I guess."

I shrugged; I knew the term, I just didn't know from where.

"What's this about?" she asked as she carefully positioned the bandage in the same manor she would hang a panting.

"Oh, it's just something I heard Dexter say once?"

She shrugged and wiped a stray strand of hair off her face. Suddenly she lit up and snapped her fingers.

"Audrey Hepburn," she said with delight.

"What?"

"That was the play. They turned it into that musical with Audrey Hepburn: *My Fair Lady*. We should watch it."

Something inside me groaned.

"Yeah, sure."

That didn't help me much. I had seen the movie years ago, but all I could remember was some professor giving a low-class Hepburn lessons on becoming a proper lady. And something about rain in Spain. Somehow I didn't think that was what was on Dexter's mind when he left that note for himself. I pushed the thought aside. Maybe it didn't matter.

Claire took my hand and led me into the living room. She looked doe-eyed, almost sad, and I knew that she was about to tell me something I didn't want to hear.

"So, do you remember what's happening next Tuesday?"

I did. I rolled my eyes.

"Your art show."

"And you're going to come this time, right?"

I hesitated. It wasn't like I didn't enjoy art, or didn't like art galleries, or even that I couldn't appreciate a painting. I just didn't like having to do it with other people. The crowd at these events was always too pretentious. I could think of a lot of other things I'd rather do with my evening.

When I didn't answer right away she went on the attack.

"Come on, you said you would after you missed the last one."

She had all but jumped in the air like a kid who had just been told she couldn't have ice cream for dinner.

It made me laugh.

"Hold on, I didn't say, 'I wasn't going.'"

She playfully pushed me onto the couch.

"You didn't say anything, which is sometimes the same thing."

"Is your brother going?" I asked.

Her hands went up defensively.

"I know what you think about Chris, but–"

"Claire, honey, he hates me."

"That's what I'm talking about. He doesn't hate you."

"I don't want to argue about this right now," I sighed.

"Then let's not argue. Just pick me up at five."

She crawled into my lap and kissed my cheek.

I smiled.

"Thank you," she added.

"I didn't actually say, 'yes.'"

She looked up at me and smiled. "You didn't say anything, which is the same thing."

I gave her a firm squeeze, but I felt her body stiffen under my arms. I looked down to see her frown. I followed her eye line to the blanket shoved between my couch cushion's cracks. We had almost shared a tender moment, but now that was over.

"You're not still sleeping on this dirty old thing, are you?" She pushed away from me.

"Sometimes I take naps."

"Jack, you have a perfectly good bed." She motioned to the bedroom. She looked disappointed in me.

"They're just naps."

Not entirely a lie considering my sleeping habits.

She sighed and frowned; she didn't believe me. I wouldn't have believed me. But Claire wouldn't press. She changed the subject.

Now, sitting on couch next to me, with her arms crossed, she asked, "How was your day?"

I pondered the question for a moment. How could I answer it? My day had been terrible. I couldn't stop thinking about Dexter. I couldn't stop thinking about my dead wife. I'd gone over to Dexter's looking for answers, and ended up with glass in my head.

Could I tell Claire all that? Could I tell her how tormented I felt? How I was always racked with guilt and grief? Certainly she wouldn't judge me. If anything, revealing my feelings to her might actually help us grow closer together. It would enable us to relate with one another on a more intimate level.

So I lied.

"It was okay," I said.

"What did you do?"

I cleared my throat.

"Dex had some design documents hidden somewhere in his office, so I had to sort through some of his mess."

"Did you find what you were looking for?"

"No."

That lie was actually true.

"How was your day?" I asked.

"Fine. I ran a bunch of errands, and then I went…"

She tilted her head back and it looked like she was holding back tears.

"Why lie about it, Jack. I'm not doing fine."

She got up and moved over to one of my apartment's windows. I stood to follow. I wanted to comfort her, but didn't feel comfortable about it. I was shamed that she could confess her true feelings and I couldn't.

"I drove by Dexter's place after work," she said.

"Really? W-what were you doing there?"

I'd asked the question reflexively, and then cringed. I hoped it didn't sound nearly as rude or intrusive to her. If she had gone over to Dexter's house she must have seen my car. I had been there practically all day. But she didn't challenge me on the subject – didn't question what I had been doing there. She just cried.

She turned to face me with a furrowed expression that was something like a smile and a lot like sorrow.

"I miss him too Jack."

Light from the streetlamps haloed her dark hair and glinted off the tears on her cheek. Her taut skin radiated a soft glow. Her beauty was celestial. I swallowed my lust.

"I couldn't go in," she continued. "They had the front door taped off, but I just wanted to see the place. I felt like I needed to. You know?"

Her expression faded, and I knew she was there again. She was looking at his front door. She had traveled back in time and was staring at the sullen frame covered in police tape.

"I'm sorry," I said in a dry, even tone.

Then she was looking at me again, giving me a wet smile.

"I keep trying to recall all the memories I have of him. I want to remember everything I can about Dexter. Now that there won't be any new memories, I want to make sure all the time we spent together is kept somewhere precious. You know what I mean?"

"Yeah, I do." I said.

She pointed to one of my bookshelves.

"This one time, I let him borrow Eco's *The Name of the Rose*. I told him it was one of the greatest novels ever written, and he said he'd always wanted to read it. But then a few weeks later, he admitted that he didn't like it."

She chuckled at the memory.

"As he started to explain why – started to point out parts of the narrative he had problems with – I realized that I didn't know what he was talking about. I hardly remembered the story at all. This is one of my favorite books, and it was almost like I'd never read it."

I grunted some kind of acknowledgment.

"So here is what I have been thinking," she continued. "I have walls of bookcases at my house. Millions of pages from

Shakespeare to Steven King. I have a stack higher than my house that I can stand on and claim I've read, but if I don't remember them, what does it matter? If you can't trust your memories, are they important?"

She was on the verge of breaking down. I wanted to console her, but she was on the other side of the room.

"Claire I–"

"I've been trying to remember Dexter – trying to collect every memory, but I can't hold them all in my head at once. I feel like I'm missing so many. It makes me wonder if there is a point to remembering at all."

She wiped tears from her face as she sniffled.

"What is the point, Jack?"

I was not the person to ask. I had spent the past couple years avoiding that question.

"I think Dexter would have wanted us to remember the good things, rather than dwell on what's gone."

I had pulled that answer out of my ass. I didn't think it actually meant anything – not to me. It didn't even sound that good. It was trite. Hollow. It felt like an empty greeting card the day after your birthday. How was I supposed to give her a comforting answer when I was still agonizing over the question myself?

For that matter, how was I supposed to know how Dexter wanted us to react to his suicide? I know what he might have wanted, but he had become a different man since I last saw him. The act of taking his own life had transformed him. I didn't know the Dexter who killed himself. I may have known a Dexter with opportunity, who never acted. But in those final moments – right after he had made a commitment to death and just before he'd actually breathed his last – Dexter experienced something that I hadn't. I couldn't even guess at what he thought or believed in after that experience?

He was selfish enough to go there alone. I envied him for it. Dexter had gone to an extreme to avoid the question Claire had just asked me. Or perhaps his death was a result of an answer I might never understand. Maybe he had even found an answer during those last few seconds before the black. I hoped he was that lucky. Whatever happened during his last beat of life, he died as a man I no longer knew, and he had taken his answers with him.

"I think what really matters," I said. "Is that Dexter would want us to keep living with his memories."

Claire shook her head and sighed, but I couldn't tell whether or not she knew I was full of shit. She walked into my arms. I noticed soggy bags under her eyes, pink from wiping away tears all day. She squeezed them and a river of mascara trickled down her cheeks.

"Why do we have to keep going through this?" she asked.

The memory was on me in a flash. Hot and fast. My own personal disaster in vivid, multidimensional detail. I heard the muted explosion reverberating through the years. The acrid sulfur stole my breath – it suffocated me. Fiery rubies floated through the air. Like seeds in the wind, my wife's blood hovered in front of me. I would never forget this snapshot of death.

Claire was wrong. I hadn't been through this before. The last time had been much worse.

"Claire…" but what could I say. "Let's not talk about that."

We sat down on the couch in silence. I held her for a long time. Our relationship had been non-sexual for a long time. It was something that most people wouldn't understand, but it made things easier for both of us.

Eventually Claire fell asleep in my arms. I lay awake with a mass of knots tightening in my chest. I couldn't sleep. Dexter's suicide had knocked me off my treadmill of avoidance, and now my wife's memory was catching up. Two years of well-buried emotions unearthed in a matter of days. I'd never buried her along with her body. Her ghost would come calling soon, and there would be a reckoning.

0101000001010010010001010101010011010100110010000001010011010101
0001000001010100100101010000100000101010001001111
00100000010000110100111101001110010
10100010010010100110010
1010101000101

CHAPTER SIX: PRESS START TO CONTINUE

Shoes crunch over dry grass.

Hey babe.

…

I … I brought you flowers.

Paper crumples against stone.

Say hi to Dexter for me.

A weak laugh.

I try to smile for you sometimes, but my face won't obey.

Sniff.

I really needed you today. It was worse than it has been in a long time.

The noiseless fall of tears.

Things aren't going well with Claire.

I don't know how much longer we're going to last…she knows my heart's not in it…

I just wish you were here, babe.

I…

I'm sorry it ended this way.

I'm so sorry.

A body rocks hard with sorrow. Approaching footfalls. The weeping takes no pause.

Who are you?

A thousand voices scream!

No! You can't take her. If you need someone take me instead.
A thousand voices scream!
Wait! I changed my mind. Don't take me away from her.
No! Stop pulling me. I can't breathe, it hurts!
…
Wait, what is that?
A rustling of chains. A low growl.
How did you get that? That's my secret place. You have no right to
touch it.
A thousand voices whisper.
Don't let him out. He's dangerous. That's why he's caged.
…
No, you can't. You don't know what you're doing. Stop!
A lock opens with a quick click. A door hinge creaks
slowly open.
Powerful silence.
A thousand voices wail and gnash their teeth.
NO! NO! NO!

01000101010101011001001001

"…no."

I awoke heaving in my living room. The screams of my
night terror transformed into hoarse gasps as the white
world of my mind folded back into a dust-covered reality.
My couch was a mess, its pillows tossed across the room.
The single blanket I normally used for warmth was drenched
in a sick sweat. It lay twisted up around my feet. My life is a
nightmare that's only worse when I'm awake.

Insomnia. It has nothing to do with the number of hours
you sleep; it's defined by the quality of rest you receive. It's a
condition ten percent of the population suffers in some
chronic form. I'd been that ten percent for over two years.

I looked around, half expecting to see my wife's
headstone in a corner, and thankful I didn't find a caged
monster. One image from my dream remained more vivid
than the others: the man who had unlocked the cage. A man

with reversed eyes – white pupils and black sclera. A man with green irises that flashed as he spoke...no...when he talked without sound. A man who might have been death.

A man who might have been something worse than death.

I looked out my window. Dawn was infecting the sky. It was 6:03 am, still too early for a programmer to be productive, but too late to go back to sleep. I got up and walked around my apartment. Claire was long gone, vanishing during some peaceful period of the night.

In the mornings, my apartment scares me. I am haunted by hollow memories. Near-fantasies of the way life should have been. A woman's laughter echoes off the walls. I see her reflection in a picture of dolphins that sits in my bathroom. There is a living absence in my bedroom – sometimes it manifests like a ghost.

But the morning after the break-in at Dexter's, I was distracted by pain. The memory of my dream was starting to fade into a migraine. Every footfall against my tufted carpet poked through my feet and pinched my skull. I walked into the bathroom, and, out of habit, turned on the light. I regretted it immediately, and flipped the switch back off. My tongue looked like a petri dish from the center for disease control, so I brushed it carefully, suppressing a strong desire to heave. A handful of Aspirin later, I was in the shower.

The soothing pound of water was the cure for many of my neck's angry muscles. Soon my migraine subsided into a mild throb. Unfortunately, other parts of my body had complaints to voice: the spider crack on my head and the swelling welt on my shin. The bruise on my leg had gotten worse overnight, and I decided to take more medication, exceeding "my daily recommended amount." I didn't care.

Unfortunately, neither did the pain.

The events of the night before continued to consume me. I couldn't stop thinking about Dexter's Evi program. Was it possible that I had imagined much of the experience? It wasn't uncommon for insomniacs to hallucinate. Maybe Evi had been little more than the lucid dream of a sleep-deprived man.

I pushed the thought out of my head. I wasn't going crazy; I just needed something to stabilize myself. I needed a break. I needed to escape my life for a bit. Fortunately, escape was something I owned in spades.

I burrowed deep.

Most of the stuff in my apartment – from my college bookshelves to the couch I slept on every night – was years old and from another life. But I had spent thousands of dollars to make sure my entertainment setup was high-end and brand new. I owned a 50" rear-projection TV, a Dolby Digital five channel home theater sound system, and the three city blocks worth of cords necessary to hook it all up to every video game system that had hit the market in the last two decades.

I called it a hobby, but my collection of obscure video game memorabilia resembled an obsession. But, provided I perpetually fed this dysfunction, it supplied me with short-lived joy.

I owned dozens of home video consoles, some of them rare, like my Brazilian version of the Japanese MSX computer, or my two broken 1977 RCA Studio IIs, or my NEC PC-Engine, which was just the older Japanese brother to the TurboGraphx-16. The first system I ever owned – a Commodore 64 – sat awkwardly next to my 200 MHz PC, which I had overclocked to keep up with some of the more demanding PC titles on the market. I also had well over 1000 games, and my eagerness to display them made my meager apartment feel more cramped than it should. I liked to believe that I was preserving video game history, but it was all trash compared to what I'd lost.

The only downside to having this many diversions at hand, was picking one to play. Today was an exception. The image of Dexter's corpse was too firmly burrowed into my consciousness, and I was determined to beat the nested memory out of my skull. Today, I wanted to pick a fight.

I slid *Virtua Fighter 2* off of one of my gaming shelves and turned on my Sega Saturn.

If every game was its own little world, then *Virtua Fighter* was a world with its own special language. It was the simplest language of all: speech without words. *Virtua Fighter* was a dialogue of fists and feet.

Most fighting games can be beaten in an hour or less, and *Virtua Fighter* was no exception, but the point of a fighting game has never been to just to beat it. The point is to master it – to become such an expert in the language that you feel immortal. Like any real martial art, this requires rote practice.

In *Virtua Fighter*, I was a master. Before long I had worked my way to the end of the game. Then, suddenly, I hit a wall.

Her name was Dural. She looked as though she had been poured from liquid metal, and her body glimmered with a mirror's sheen. Every extraneous edge to the human figure had been sanded away. Dural had been built for only one task: victory. She was elegant simplicity; a pure fighter.

We took our positions and the signal to fight was given. It was time for us to debate with violence. I started the match with a simple punch kick combo. It was promptly dodged, and I was bombarded with a flurry of counter attacks so fast I couldn't deflect them. Before I knew it, the match was over.

"K.O.," roared an animated disembodied voice. "You Lose," appeared on screen in bold red, as though I didn't already know what had happened. When the question, "Continue?" popped up, I pressed start and jumped back into the game. It was my first loss. It hardly fazed me.

The second time I started with a Jumping Kick and followed through with a Single Palm Mouko Kouhazan attack. My opponent was too well-trained, and she reversed my attacks effortlessly. Again, the match was over before I realized it.

"K.O."

You Lose.

Continue?

Thankfully, in this world, every hero was given an endless supply of opportunity with which to rise above his betters. True heroics were not measured by the level of one's skill, but by the determination of one's will. In this world, I was a superman – a phoenix – capable of rising from defeat as many times as it took me to achieve victory.

"Any monkey can get lucky once or twice," I told the screen.

I altered my tactics and went on the defensive. Straight out of the gate I was subjected to a frontal Toka throw. I never recovered.

"K.O." You Lose. Continue?

Every match I tried something new. A Sokutai Side Kick into a Jyoho Chouchuu Elbow Strike. Blocked. Rakugeki Sousui Jumping Hammer. Parried. Even the extremely complex Hougeki Unshin Soukoshou Stun Palm Combo. Sidestepped. It didn't matter what I tried; I always ended up staring at the same screen.

"K.O." You Lose. Continue?

I was through being patient with myself; I was a better virtual fighter than this. I had beaten this game dozens of times before. What was my problem now? I fumed at myself for not being fast enough, for not being cautious enough, for being too reckless. I cursed at the controller for not obeying my commands.

The AI had one advantage I did not. It didn't just exist within the code, it was code. I imagined that it was like being aware of everything that happened all at once. I observed the world one second at a time through a single slit of screen, but the AI had an intimate three dimensional knowledge of her surroundings, and she processed every pixel of it at the speed of electric thought.

She would always be faster. She would always be stronger. She would always be more determined, more energetic, and somehow, always have at least an ounce of endurance more than me.

I didn't feel powerful anymore. I couldn't overcome this problem. My movements were too limited. I wanted to quit. Then Dexter flashed through my head, and I knew I couldn't abandon him. He needed me; I was fighting for him.

I had failed him the first time. I had failed to prevent him from taking his own life. I should have foreseen it; I should have recognized the signs and done something.

This was my chance to redeem myself. This battle was more than recreation. I wasn't displaying my skills for a digitized trophy or an abstract concept like honor. I wasn't fighting a computer whose actions were determined by algorithms pre- programmed years before I'd put this disc in my system; I was fighting for Dexter's life.

Lost in a storm of guilt-drunk emotion – something like a personal breakdown – I realized that I was opposing Death itself. I was fighting to undo Dexter's tragedy. To undo my mistake. To bring back the dead. This was an intangible battle, an impossible war. And yet, I was possessed by a rage that told me I could win.

My opponent had demonstrated greater skill in the ring, so I would have to prove that my will was stronger. I prepared once more for combat. Any monkey can get lucky once, I prayed.

Athletes talk about moments where their whole body functions with complete synergy – it's a period in time where their thoughts and their actions become one. There is no wasted energy, only perfect motion. They call it being "in the zone." I had just arrived there.

From my couch, I directed every motion of combat as though I were a puppet master. All my combos, all my attacks, all my strategies flowed seamlessly together. The sounds of the world around me lagged as they tried to keep up with my precision. My virtual self and I became one; we were extensions of each other. No longer were we separated by the controller in my hands. It became a tether binding us – our umbilical. I dwindled my opponent's life down to a sliver. For a moment I couldn't be touched. In that one moment, I couldn't lose.

Then there was a slip.

A memory: the yellow crack of an open door, the flash of a gun barrel under an orange sunset, red blood on pale skin. A memory. My wife's memory.

Death began to match me at every move. Her attacks started to sink through my defenses. My own movements were no longer smooth – no longer firm. I couldn't beat Death, I realized. I had already lost to her two years ago.

"K.O." You Lose. Continue?

Defeat felt real this time, but I was too emotionally exhausted to cry out, and too physically worn down to throw the controller. The game-world illusion was broken. "K.O. You Lose. Continue?" no longer felt like another opportunity to win. It felt like another way of saying, "Give up yet?"

My purpose for fighting evaporated as I accepted two truths. The people I had once loved were dead. And I was powerless to do anything about it.

For the next several hours, I continued to play anyway. I let the emotional press of defeat push me deeper into my couch. I didn't retain any hope of victory. Winning wouldn't really bring anyone back to life. I was tired. I was suffering form sleep deprivation. My brain had reached its limit and was beginning to crack. But continuing to lose like I did was a disturbed behavior; it was my masochistic way of cutting myself.

Eventually I felt so exhausted, beaten, and abandoned that I rolled over on my couch. The alarm I kept nearby began to chirp. It was time to get ready for work. I didn't care. My last match ended just like all the others. Just like Dexter's personal battle had ended. Just like everything had ended two years ago.

"K.O." You Lose. Continue?

CHAPTER SEVEN: LIVING STONE

When Dexter and I first started looking for office space for our studio, it quickly evolved into a kind of competition to see who could find a location closer to his own apartment. I found some great space on the eighth floor of a building only three blocks from my apartment in downtown San Francisco. It was better than anything Dexter could dig up. I won. My prize was getting to walk to work everyday.

Some days I could hear our receptionist, Amy, talking on the phone as I exited the elevator. The day after my confrontation with the shadowy figure in Dexter's house, I strolled into the office a little after noon. Amy was on the phone with an irate parent.

"Well, I'm sorry to hear that your child's grades have suffered because he's playing too many games, but–"

The angry warble of the woman on the other end cut her off.

"Ma'am please, I know for a fact that the developers did not hide any satanic messages in the game–"

The garbled voice rose angrily. I almost smiled. God bless that woman.

Amy looked up from the phone to see me pass by. She tried to motion me over. I ignored her, and the last thing I heard before I turned a corner into the bullpen was an exasperated receptionist squeak out, "Because I work for them."

ESP's offices (Dexter's "clever" acronym for our company), was mostly open space. Dexter's office sat in one corner of the building, and mine was tucked into the other. Aside from the art department's room – which ran between our offices – the floor was one large bullpen. Six scattered support pillars diminished some of its size, but ESP retained an open atmosphere.

We'd fit comfortably into this space when we were working on our first game, but there were only a dozen of us back then. Our numbers had almost tripled now that we were developing our third title, and the space was getting cramped. Back in the '80s, one programmer could make an entire game by himself in a few months, I was almost sad I'd missed that era.

As I hurried toward my office, I avoided the gaze of dozens of employees. Normally, they enjoyed watching me show up late to work, but today I noticed an uncomfortable pity behind their stares. The news of Dexter's death had finally leaked. I hadn't meant for it too. I'd wanted to tell the staff myself, but Dexter's father had been so proactive in funeral planning that he'd called the office early that morning and given Amy details about the reception. Amy thought it was a joke at first, but the information had quickly spread through the bullpen. Just before I'd left the apartment, that morning, I'd started to get calls from member of our staff who wanted to know what was going on. I called Amy to let everyone know that they could take the day off. Half the staff already had; the other half looked like they would be out the door in a few minutes.

I don't really know why I even bothered going into the office that day. I think I needed the routine. I couldn't stand my apartment, and I didn't have anywhere else to go.

Gordon, ESP's heavyset art director, yelled at me from across the bullpen as I opened my office door.

"Hey, Jack! We have the art for The Shrine all finished. Can you come approve it?"

One of the programmers that Gordon had been talking with gave him a smack on the arm that said, "Maybe you should leave him alone." Gordon looked at him with a startled shrug that said, "What's the problem?"

"I just got in," I said. "Is it an emergency?"

"If I say 'no' will you still come check it out?"

"Give me a few minutes," I sighed.

Gordon pleaded with clasped hands. "Please Jack, today. We're behind schedule."

"When have I ever blown you off?" I said with a weak smile before turning my back on him and entering my office.

"You mean this week?" he called out sarcastically.

I closed my door.

When Dexter and I first envisioned making a game together we wanted to build a company that utilized both our strengths. Dexter was one of the most talented programmers I had ever known, so he handled the technical guts of all our games. All the programming issues, such as how many polygons we could push onscreen at once, were his responsibility. My job was lead designer. I had to make our games fun.

I'm convinced he got the easy part.

Fun isn't an easily value to measure. There's no formula for joy. While I found it easy to point at something I enjoyed, it was much harder to shape a similar experience from the ground up. A good portion of my time was spent inside our games, playing them and adjusting level layouts to make sure that object and enemy placement was fine-tuned for every difficulty, and generally trying to create a digital experience that would shepherd players smoothly through all the major gaming events.

With so many different games, movies, books, and sports continually reshaping our cultural consciousness, fun was a moving target. But that was why I was content with the weak performance of ESP's first title. While our first game had received some critical praise, it hadn't sold nearly as well has we would have liked. Now we were in early development of our untitled third game. We desperately needed it to be a hit.

On top of all the pressure to be entertaining, ESP still needed to function like a business. As a designer I had to have a clear vision of what our games would ultimately look like, and then I needed to clearly communicate that dream to the whole team. It had become my unofficial job to coordinate traffic between the different departments. My life was ripe with meetings, but even armed with schedules, planners, and spreadsheets I was in a constant battle to keep everyone on track. Amidst the onrush of ever encroaching deadlines, I'd long since given up on keeping my office tidy.

I looked at my desk. I didn't know where to begin. I had a stacks of level design changes to go over, a couple of unreturned phone messages about sound effect samples, and a list of bug reports to follow up on. I was falling behind more than ever. But I honestly didn't feel like working. I tried shifting around the stacks on my desk for a minute then fumbled with a couple unlabeled floppy discs when I saw a note that Gordon had left on my desk the day before.

The note read, "Finished the art for Shrine. Had to change Pygmalion's statue a bit, but come take a look at it when you have a chance."

There was the Pygmalion reference again – the same word that I'd seen at Dexter's house the night before. It seemed like a strange coincidence. I stood and walked out to the bullpen. It was nearly empty now. Two programmers huddled over one monitor. I didn't see Gordon.

But I could hear Gordon talking over in the art department.

"So he said to me, 'why don't you go find the spec sheet?'"

"He really said that?" I heard someone else whisper.

I poked my head into the art department's large room.

Gordon sat at his desk, chewing a piece of licorice. He was talking with one of our associate concept artists, a gangly, long-haired kid named Dante.

"So," Gordon continued. "I said to him: 'I know what we can do; let's find out what the boss thinks?'"

Gordon acted out the scene, motioning dramatically at the name plaque on his desk then looking back at Dante in mock surprise.

"Well look at this! This says, 'I'm the art director.'"

Dante chuckled.

"'And since you're the art intern, I guess, I get to tell you what to do. So start sorting through the filing cabinets and find me that spec sheet.'"

The art department had a reputation for being crazier than the rest of the company. I'd once heard the phrase "If you want to eat my shoe, you'll have to hunt it and kill it first," echo out of the room. I was lucky enough to wander into a conversation that made sense.

Gordon paused his story to pull out another strand of licorice. At over 300 pounds, Gordon was a harmless bear. He was outspoken, blunt, and slightly narcissistic, yet people couldn't help but like him. He had a disarming sense of humor that made almost everyone laugh – and in the most impressive displays of his power – sometimes at themselves. His brain was a warehouse of science-fiction and pop-culture. And his I-know-everything-and yes-I-can-prove-it attitude made him extremely good at his job.

"And then what?" Dante asked snorting.

Dante was a sidekick.

"He quit. Just walked out the front door right then," Gordon finished. "The sad part was that I didn't actually need the spec sheet," Gordon said sarcastically. "It was all just part of my evil Machiavellian power play."

Dante cracked up hysterically. I thought the story was amusing, but it was well over a year old, and I'd probably heard it a half dozen times. I think Dante had too. But Dante liked to be amused.

I cleared my throat, and the duo looked up. I held up the note Gordon had left on my desk and opened my mouth to speak, but Gordon didn't give me the opportunity.

"Oh, yeah, over there," he pointed to an open computer in the corner of the room. "Prepare to be blown away."

"Or just blown," Dante giggled immaturely.

Gordon acted like he hadn't heard him and swiveled around to face his monitor. I quietly walked over to the open computer and sat down. The room was peacefully silent, but Gordon didn't let that last long.

"You know what this room needs? Some snappier dialogue." He began snapping his fingers. "That would really spice up the place."

Dante let out a belly laugh.

Again, I wondered why I had even bothered coming into the office.

I focused on the wire mesh model in front of me. The environment of the level was constructed out of geometric polygons – the basic math used to build everything in artificial 3D space. I pulled up the artwork associated with the shapes, and Shrine popped into existence.

In the background, I could see the ashes of one of Greece's ancient, war-torn cities. Rubble filled the empty streets. Eventually, we would set the city on fire, adding flicker lighting to the interior of many of its buildings and painting the skies with smoke, but much of that work still had to be done, and the stillness gave this area an eerie sadness. The city looked broken, yet quiet. As I looked across the center of the level I was overcome by an unnatural emotion. The same feeling of being watched that I'd experienced the night before, at Dexter's house.

I pushed it aside.

The level's most notable feature was an open courtyard featuring a large fountain. A beautiful ivory woman, in true Grecian splendor, rested in the pool's center. The courtyard itself contained multiple entry-points for enemies, but only one correct exit for the player. I knew this level's layout well. I'd designed it.

In many ways, good game design is about control, which is funny because most people believe that the player is in control of a game. After all, they are the ones holding the controller. But that's a deception; one that game makers work very hard to maintain. Despite their freedom, players are really being led along by the invisible hand of a designer.

The freedom of player's choice is trumped by a greater need – the need to have fun. Anyone who picks up a game wants to feel like they are affecting the world, but they also want to feel like they are moving through a story. The trick to keeping both in balance is anticipating a player's reaction during almost any given situation, and then placing the workable solutions in front of them in such a way that they feel like they've discovered it. It means telling players what to do without directly telling them what to do.

Shrine's courtyard was a Gate – a designer's term for anything that halts a player's progress. Anyone playing our game would be contained inside this fountain area until they initiated the Gate's puzzle, at which point the courtyard would swarm with enemies. Leaving the arena empty on arrival served to mount tension and allow players to get a lay of the land before being forced into a fight. Dexter disagreed with this tactic. He wanted to keep throwing enemies at players, but I've always believed that pacing is an important part of any medium, even the most twitch video game.

"Hey, Gordon?" I shouted without looking over my shoulder.

"Hey, Bossman?" Gordon swiveled in his chair, making five tiny steeples with the points of his fingers.

"You're note mentioned that you had to change some of the artwork for Pygmalion's statue." I asked without really making it a question.

"Ah, the great Shrine dilemma," Gordon said with sarcastic fondness. "Dexter wanted a specific design for the fountain, but the model took up too much memory."

"This is the new design?" I said pointing at my monitor.

"Yeah that's it; Galatea's new skin."

"Galatea?" I asked.

"That's her name," Dante chimed in. "She's some kind of Roman goddess."

"She's not really a goddess," Gordon corrected. "She's from the Greek myth of Pygmalion."

I looked back at the statue on my monitor with newfound interest. It had been Dexter's idea to include little snippets of Greek myth in our games.

I turned back to Gordon. He had pulled out his lunch bag and placed a small yellow container on the work table in the middle of the room.

"What are you doing?" Dante asked.

"Remember how we were having problems finding a good design for our walls in the Homunculi cave?"

"Yeah."

"Well this is our cave."

Gordon gave a dramatic flourish as he pulled the plastic cover off a Tupperware container, releasing a foul odor. Dante coughed and fanned the air from his nose. Inside Gordon's container sat a molded, possibly frostbitten slice of meatloaf.

"Where's the old art?" I interrupted, asking about the Shrine statue.

"We never found anything we were happy with, but don't worry this will work."

"No," I corrected, "I mean, where is the old art Dexter wanted to use for the Galatea?"

But Dante was eager to ask questions too. "What is it?" he asked, pointing at the ugly meat.

Gordon adjusted the scanning equipment on the big table in front of him.

"Well, last month it was dinner. This week it's a living cave wall."

"Uh, Gordon," I said trying to contain my eagerness.

"You know, it actually looks way better than anything we drew," Dante said pinching his nose.

I had watched these guys put everything from rusted metal, to body parts, to live bugs into our games, and the results always turned out great. They had an eye for making games look good. I trusted them, but I was more interested in Dexter's old art for the Shrine statue.

Gordon looked up at me. He was so lost in his work that it took him a few beats to remember my question from less than fifteen seconds before.

"Shrine art?" he said rubbing his face. "Uh…we still have it. Do you need to see it right now?" he asked with a frown.

"When you have a free second," I tried to say patiently.

"Can it wait until tomorrow?" Gordon asked immediately turning back to his equipment.

It wasn't really a question, but I decided it could wait.

"Sure."

As I was leaving, I shoved my hands in my pocket and something bit my pinkie. With a yelp, I withdrew my hand. A firm rectangle of paper fluttered to the floor. The thin sheet had slipped under my fingernail, giving me a bloody paper cut. I reached down to pick up the object while I sucking the blood out of the tip of my hand. It was the business card I'd unwittingly pocketed from Dexter's house the night before. The card read:

> Professor Hironobu Hojo
> Stanford University
> Department of Computer Science
> Professor (Research), Computer Science Department
> June '86 to present.
> Co-Scientific Director, Knowledge Systems Laboratory

"What's that?" Dante asked noisily.

I flipped the card around in my hand as though a through examination of the object would help me explain it.

"It's a business card. I, uh, guess it's someone that Dexter knew. This guy, this…" I read the card again. "Professor Hojo."

"Have you called him? Does he know what happened to Dexter?"

"I don't know," I looked up embarrassed. "I…I sort of forgot I had this."

"We could look him up on the net," Gordon jumped in.

Before I could respond he'd snatched the card from my hand, spun his chair over to his computer, and started dialing into AOL. Gordon liked to boast about how he occasionally performed "professional-level" hacking during his free time. I never questioned him. He surfed the internet so much, it might as well have been his job.

"Don't bother; it's not that important," I said.

Gordon didn't flinch.

"How did Dexter know this guy?" Dante asked.

"Seriously Gordon, we don't need to look this guy up," I said.

But AOL was already piecing its search page together.

Gordon raised a finger. "This won't take long."

I sighed; it was out of my hands.

"How did Dexter know this guy?" Dante asked again.

"I don't know," I confessed. "I found the card at Dexter's place the other day."

"And that's all you know?"

"Well, yeah."

"Okay, so what makes you think they know each other?"

Dante rubbed the back of his neck; he always took a nervous posture whenever he questioned someone's idea.

"He could have gotten that business card any number of ways." He started counting them off on his hand. "A mutual acquaintance, a seminar, the mail–"

"The mail?" I asked with a smirk. "Is it the time of year when the professors start mailing out their cards already? I haven't gotten mine yet."

Dante shrugged.

"The trash," Gordon blurted out while pounding away at his keyboard.

"The trash," Dante echoed earnestly as though that idea were actually less ridiculous than his had been – as though Dexter regularly rescued random business cards from the trash. He even underlined the statement with a pointed finger.

I rubbed my temples; I could only take so much art department in one day. I had grabbed the business card from Dexter's desk on a whim. That was all. I'd forgotten all about it until it drew blood.

"Okay, I've got something," Gordon shouted from a distance of two feet.

Dante and I leaned over his shoulder. A low resolution image slowly un-scroll from the top of the monitor. We could start to see a balding, mid-fiftyish Asian gentleman. He wore a brown Mr. Roger's jacket and a stern pout.

Gordon quickly scanned the page's text.

"Professor Hironobu Hojo…Born in Osaka, Japan in 1963…Moved to England with his family when he was seven…An Oxford man, hmm. Majored in Engineering and Computer Systems, and then…moved to the states to teach. Well traveled guy…Divorced. But there is a picture of him with his daughter."

Dante nudged forward.

"Is she hot?"

Gordon shot him a pious look that said "heel," and Dante backed off a little ashamed. I'd definitely had enough art department.

"Here are his office hours, but…" Gordon scrolled down. "It looks like he's leaving on sabbatical next week."

A sabbatical; what the hell did that mean? Who in this day and age actually took a sabbatical?

"A sabbatical!" Dante said, "What the hell does that mean?"

Gordon offered an answer. "It's when someone takes an extended period of leave from–"

"I know what it means," Dante said defensively. "People still do that?"

"You might be able to catch him this afternoon," Gordon said turning to me. "You want the address?"

I hesitated. It seemed a little ridiculous. There were probably a dozen reasons why I shouldn't bother trucking halfway across the city to talk with a professor who may or may not have known my dead friend. It was crazy. And yet I could feel a hunger stirring in my gut. I was reminded just how little I knew about Dexter's death. How could I resist a lead that literally fell in my lap? The junior Sherlock Holmes inside me had already walked out the door, telling Watson to grab his gun.

"Print it off," I said.

CHAPTER EIGHT: EVI

"It hurts to breath after you drown," she says.

I know what she means. When I was eleven my grandfather took me sailing off the coast of his Branford, Connecticut home. We got caught in a storm, and our boat capsized—

She stops me there. She's heard the story several times.

I spoon Jell-O into her mouth, and in a raspy, listless voice she tells me that she loves me.

My only response is a thin smile.

Her face disappears in a flash of static. It is replaced with a different face: one that still belongs to her, but is somehow different. She's paler. Little black ribbons stream from her eyes. We're in the car now. An endless highway lies in front of us. White hills stretch to infinity.

I see her breath as she speaks.

"Why don't you love me anymore?"

The car loses its traction on a frozen road. It's out of my control. Her face opens into a scream as the car collides with something bigger and less mobile. Metal tears open like a demons mouth, and it swallows me whole.

A hand pressed on my shoulder. Someone was calling me back to life. My head rolled forward slightly, and my neck muscles immediately screamed out in pain. Drowsily, I looked around. I was sitting on a poorly finished wooden bench. It must have been the most uncomfortable seat ever crafted by human hands.

"Are you okay, sir?"

I looked up to see a curly, silver-haired woman towering over me.

"I'm fine."

But my cracked voice and sweaty brow didn't convince either of us.

I tried to shake myself out of my insomnia episode, but reality was coming back slowly. The world felt still. I could hear the hum of a computer twenty feet away. It took me a moment to remember were I was, or why I was there. I was sitting on a bench inside the William Gates Computer Science Building at Stanford University.

It was a terrible place to take a nap.

"You asked me to let you know when Professor Hojo returned," said the woman above me.

I stared at her blankly.

"He just walked upstairs to his office."

I grunted some version of "thank you," and the woman above me walked away looking slightly concerned.

It took me a few moments to muster up the energy to push myself off the bench. I couldn't suppress the groan necessary to exert that much energy. I had gone too long without real sleep, and a few minutes of accidental rest had only reminded me of how desperately I needed more. My muscles burned with lactic acid as they forced a body made out of sand down a long hallway of miniscule offices and frosted glass doors.

Through bleary eyes I looked out a nearby window. A thin strip of pavement ran along a grassy knoll. I would have thought a college campus would be busy with activity, but from this narrow slit the world looked empty.

I knocked on the professor's door. There was no answer. I cracked it open, and stuck my head through. A tiny man sat in a small office filled with antiques and hundreds of overflowing books. With his back to me, he scribbled furiously at a desk stuffed to the brim with papers. He made no effort to get up or introduce himself.

"Professor Hironobu Hojo?"

He acted like he hadn't heard me. I closed the door behind me, and cleared my throat.

"Excuse me, profess—"

He held up a hand while he finished scrawling a note. He didn't look up as he spoke.

"My visiting hours are over."

His smooth English accent seemed an odd fit for this Japanese born gentleman.

"Dr. Albert Wily will be taking over my classes for the next term," he continued. "You should speak with him."

"I'm not a student, professor Hojo. I'm here about a friend of mine. Dexter Hayward, I thought that…"

The mention I mentioned Dexter's name, Hironobu pivoted to face me.

"…that maybe you knew him," I finished.

The professor eyed me for a moment.

"What did you say your name was?"

"Jack, Jack Valentine."

I stuck out my hand, but he ignored it.

"I'm sorry Mr. Valentine, but I don't think I can help you."

He turned back to his desk — back to his forceful scribbles.

He was lying.

"I'm sorry to be the one to tell you this, but Dexter is dead, sir. Can I ask how you knew him?"

This time Hironobu gave me his full attention.

"I don't know who you are, or how you found out about our project, Mr. Valentine."

He said my name with some disdain, as though he thought it didn't belong to me.

"But I didn't keep anything for you to buy, or steal, or copy. The project's been scrapped."

I held up my hands in defense.

"Whoa, wait a minute. I'm not sure what you're talking about. Dexter was my friend and colleague. I found your card in his house."

I pulled the man's blood-tipped card from my pocket as proof.

"I thought," I started. "Well, I don't know what I thought. I guess, I thought I should tell you the news, in case you knew him."

I frowned. This wasn't going the way I'd planned.

Hiro eyed me for a moment with a softening expression.

"Dexter's really dead?"

I nodded.

"What happened?"

"He uh…"

I swallowed a lump the size of my fist. I thought I was done delivering this news; I thought that dirty job was done.

"He'd been under a lot of stress, and he – uh – he killed himself."

Hironobu grunted then looked thoughtfully towards one of his bookshelves. I could have been mistaken, but he actually seemed impressed.

"You and Dexter were working on a project together?" I gently pressed.

"Yes," he said still exploring his bookshelf.

"What kind of project?"

Hiro rubbed the corners of his mouth in resignation.

"Your friend wanted my help with an artificial intelligence program."

I leaned forward.

"Seriously?"

He nodded.

"The project sounded exciting – it was right up my alley – so I took a look at it."

"This program? What was it called?"

The professor looked away silently for a moment then turned back to me.

"What was that?"

"What was the name of this AI program you helped Dexter developed?"

"I'm afraid we weren't very inventive. The original title was Evolved Virtual Intelligence. For short we called it Project–"

"Evi," I exclaimed excitedly.

"You do know about it?" Hiro asked.

"Not really, I…uh…I ran across the program while sorting Dexter effects."

His eyes went wide.

"You've seen it? Where is it now?"

I felt oddly compelled to lie; instead I told a half-truth.

"On one of Dexter's old home computers."

"You should destroy it."

"Why? What's wrong with it? What does it do?"

"Those are three entirely different questions, requiring three very involved answers."

I waited.

Hiro cleared his throat.

"Mr. Valentine, are you aware that the computing world is in desperate need of a new way to program?"

I shrugged. "No."

"We haven't come to grips with our own mortal limits yet. It's amazing that computer engineering works as well as it does. Hundreds, even thousands, of people work on software that talks to compilers written by a different set of people written decades ago, and all of this runs on hardware systems designed by a different set of engineers. No one has a truly complete view of how it all works. Redundancy programming only works on problems we can anticipate, and even then, correctly functioning programs often behave in unexpected ways. That's why programmers end up with so many software bugs."

"I'm familiar with some of those problems," I said. "I'm a bit of a programmer myself."

He ignored me.

"The point of Evi was, to not to create a program, but to create a new way of programming – one that would bypass these issues. We were trying to change the world."

"How so?"

He waved me off.

"That's a long class, and you are not my student. I wouldn't know where to begin."

But I did.

"How about the beginning?"

Hiro looked at me and smiled.

"You're a little like him aren't you?"

"Like Dexter?" I asked.

"Yes, you're both very curious."

I smiled. It was one of the best compliments I'd ever received.

"You have to go back a long ways to get to the beginning. The origin of Evi, like all programs, is built on the work of hundreds of pioneers. In the nineteenth century a logician named George Boole spelled out three basic variables, which are now used as the building blocks for all computer coding."

"Boolian logic," I said. "I'm familiar with it."

Hiro wasn't deterred. I was going to get a history lesson.

"But we can't start there, that's not the whole picture. You see in the 1600's, Dr William Gilbert investigated the reactions between amber and magnets. He was actually the first person to record the word 'electric' when he published *De Magnete*, a report on the theory of magnetism."

"Okay," I nodded.

"You see his work was built off something else. It's always built off something else. If you go further back, to around 600 BC, the Greeks discovered that straw particles were attracted to fur after the cloth had been rubbed against fossilized resin amber. Magnetic phenomena existed long before people understood the concept or even had words for it. For centuries we've been trying to figure out how the forces around us work, but all our progress is just built off the work of those who came before us."

It sounded like he was giving me one of his class lectures. It seemed like he wanted to talk; maybe he needed to talk. The man didn't seem entirely stable.

"You see, man has been creating things throughout his entire history. Before the computer came the light bulb. Before the light bulb came the printing press. Before the printing press came the clock. Humanity's desire to have a hand in creation stretches as far back as we can look, to the very dawn of time when Adam began naming animals. It's almost as though our entire race has been working towards…"

In true professorial style Hiro pointed at me as he posed his next question.

"Towards what?"

How the hell was I suppose to know?

"I don't know," I shrugged.

"The world's leading engineers and authors – history's finest philosophers and scientists have all been seeking to encode the laws of human thought into complex, logical systems that can be used to solve every sort of problem. We've been trying to distill human life into a box – a box that will do all of humanity's heavy lifting. A god box that will solve all our problems."

Was that an answer? The professor was beginning to make me nervous. I didn't know what he was talking about any more, or what any of this had to do with Dexter and his AI program.

"Are you saying human intelligence is nothing more than a complex computer system?"

"Well that questions opens up a nearly infinite number of philosophical ramifications, doesn't it?" he said smiling.

I ran my fingers through my hair. We were getting way off track.

"I'm sorry Professor, but what exactly is Evi?"

He leaned back in his chair thoughtfully.

"What is Evi? That's a good question. In the eighteenth century, a Swiss watchmaker by the name of Jaquet-Droz built an automaton call The Writer. This automated puppet could scrawl any pre-programmed sentence onto a piece of paper. With its chilling repertoire of human-like animations, the machine fascinated kings and emperors as far away as India and Japan. Rumor has it that Jaquet-Droz would even sometimes program his android to write the sentence 'Cogito ergo sum.'"

"Descartes," I said.

"Correct, the famous French philosopher's Latin phrase, 'I think therefore I am.'" Hiro nodded at me then added, "That is Evi."

"Evi is an old Swiss robot?" I asked confused.

But the professor wasn't finished schooling me.

"In 1966, Joseph Weizenbaum, a computer science professor at MIT, created a program called ELIZA. The program simulated human conversation by reposing questions using simple pattern matching rules: it was a chatterbot masquerading as a psychologist. But it fooled many into believing they were talking to a real person."

The professor pointed at me again.

"That is Evi."

"Professor Hojo, I don't think I'm following—"

He held up a single finger for me to be quiet.

"Before that, in 1936, a British logician pioneered the synthesis of two separate fields: philosophy and engineering. This mathematical genius from Cambridge University published a paper on conceptual abstract computing machines. His name was Alan Turing, and he's famous for kick starting the computer revolution. But one area of his research has been almost entirely neglected."

I took the bait. "What's that?"

"Turing had a theory that if a program – a 'child machine' if you will – could be raised into digital adulthood, than this machine would be capable of learning and even using human language intelligently. It would be a truly independent… artificial…intelligence."

The professor glared at me and pointed. I knew what was coming.

"That is Evi," he said leaning back in his chair. "It's all built on the work of others. It's all connected."

"Can we back up a second?" I asked. "So, Evi is just an AI program you guys hoped would test your theories on electronic child rearing?"

"Just an AI program! Do you understand the complexities of a thinking machine? Think of all of humankinds most impressive creations: everything from the Sistine Chapel to the Pyramids to the space shuttle. It's not just impressive that man created all these masterpieces, because even a machine can create a building or paint a picture if it has the time, the motivation, and the skill. That kind of creation is called manufacturing, Mr. Valentine. That kind of creation is programmable."

"Okay?"

"What made those achievements so spectacular – so different from any other – was the fact that their creator had the capacity to dream them up in the first place. What if we were able to create a machine that could do that? What if we could create a program that could dream? That kind of program wouldn't be 'just a program.' It would be an intelligence."

"But, that's impossible right?"

"Impossible!" Hiro laughed. "Do you even know what's impossible? We live in a world where machines fertilize our women; where virgins can have children. Soon we'll be making babies outside of the womb. We live in a world where we can put machines in our hearts to help them work. A world where we have daily conversations, through wires and satellites, with people who aren't even in the same city.

We live in a world were we genetically engineer our food, because our planets population is overextended. These things happen everyday. They're happening right now. So don't tell me what's impossible, because the definition of that word has proved somewhat elastic."

Hiro stood. He was getting very passionate and animated now. I looked passed his shoulder, and out through his window. The sun had set. Lightening flickered in the distance, and I could see the purple outlines of thick clouds. There was a storm coming. I could see it reflected clearly in the professor's eyes.

"Now, if you'll excuse me, I should be going," he said.

I stopped him at the door.

"Wait. I have to see this program again."

"I told you I can't help you. I've destroyed all my notes. Evi was a dream."

"You never keep a copy the program for yourself?"

"You misunderstand me Mr. Valentine. A program called Evi exists, but it was a disaster. It caused nothing but pain, and I destroyed it. Your friend's dream doesn't exist."

"But I don't understand. What I saw was pretty impressive—"

"Then I suggest you forget what you've seen, before it kills you like it killed your friend."

I was stunned by the idea that this program had driven Dexter to suicide. Hiro pushed past me and disappeared down the hall.

Off in the distance, the thunder rolled.

CHAPTER NINE: THE BURIED DEAD

The explosion still echoes through my mind. On quiet days – sometimes without even listening for it – I can still hear the gunshot. I can still smell the smoke in the air; still taste its residue on my tongue. In my mind, I run towards her as she falls. But even then I know she's gone.

Her name was Jill. It seemed like a perfect match. A story of legend: Jack and Jill. It was a fairytale existence. Young love, wrapped in an embrace so tight, they became one self – one life. Each half supported the other. Together meant they were complete. Together meant happiness. It was beautiful.

I failed to remember one important detail about the legend. It ends in tragedy. When one fell down, the other came tumbling after.

Her funeral was small; she didn't have much family left. Her father and mother had long since passed away, and her brother was backpacking in Tibet at the time. No aunts. No uncles. No cousins. She'd never known her grandparents, though a few friends stopped by for the service. And, of course, her sister was there.

We put *Eternally Loved and Forever Missed* on her gravestone.

I hated it.

Five words were not enough. A whole book is not enough to describe how passionately she is still loved, or how continually mourned she will forever be. I've stood in the cemetery nearly every month since, staring at the sentence inscribed on the headboard of her new bed. It's never felt right.

After her funeral, I played a game of spiritual chess, arguing with God over the injustice of her death. My fingers went numb from the cold. My face was raw from the wind. My overcoat saturated from the downpour that – as happens in all good movies about the dying – started right after we laid her body in the ground. Even then, I felt no desire to leave. I felt no desire for anything. I'd come tumbling down after.

Since then I have come to believe that it should always rain at funerals. It should rain with devotion. Rain does more than set a mood; rain mourns. It celebrates the event. I believe it is nature's way of honoring the dead with tears – a respect unmatched by the words of men.

Two years after I buried my wife, I found myself putting another body in the ground – another life I cared about. I wanted nature to express my pain. I wanted the sky to cast over, and I wanted it to rain with a blistering force that knocked over cars and uprooted trees.

I wanted the sky to bleed.

Dexter's funeral happened on a late, sunny afternoon. It was unnaturally humid; just warm enough to make wearing a suit uncomfortable. Nature was in bloom with green in every direction. There is often a surprising amount of life inside the yards where we lay our dead.

I had arrived late to the service, and received looks of shame and disgust from people I didn't know. Dexter's father had outdone himself; everything from the flowers at the service, to the church that housed them, to the casket that would soon sit six feet under, was overly garish.

Claire held my hand through the service, and handed me a tissue when I burst into tears at the gravesite. It felt strange to cry so openly in public. I hadn't done so in years, but I still remembered how. After the service was done, Claire left to fetch the car. I needed a few more minutes at the grave.

As the crowd shuffled back to the parked procession, I looked around. Several people crowded around Dexter's uncle. They shook his hand. The man probably didn't know Dexter's middle name, but he had given a twenty minute speech about his nephew's great accomplishments. I hadn't been asked to speak. On the other side of a large oak I could see David, and his assistant Emmerich, talking quietly with ESP's producer, Meryl. I couldn't help but notice Emmerich give me an uneasy stare, but I didn't know why.

Someone grabbed my arm.

"Can we talk, Jack?"

I numbly turned around. It was Shinji. We stood barely ten feet from the dirt being shoveled over Dexter's coffin.

"Sure, Shinji. How are you holding up?"

Shinji didn't look like he was taking the heat well. During the service, sweat had started to drool down his brow.

"Did Dexter...do you know if Dexter made any changes to our base code last week? Any changes to the AI or anything?"

"Huh?"

I wasn't really listening. I was still in reverie.

"I think there's a problem...I mean, I'm having problems with some of the game's code."

I rubbed my eyes. Sleep deprivation was beginning to hit me pretty hard, and work seemed like part of an altogether different life. It wasn't suitable for me to be interacting with living people.

"What do you mean?"

"Our AI constructs have started inheriting abnormal behavioral patterns," Shinji said.

"Yeah, I remember. Weren't you looking into that?"

"Well, it's worse now. They're doing some strange things," Shinji said vaguely.

"Strange things?"

"They're altering hit point values and damage ratios in order to survive longer. I'm also pretty sure I've seen them change their physical structure."

I was hearing what he was saying, but it wasn't really registering.

"Okay, I'm sure you'll figure it out—"

"None of this is possible, Jack! They're creating art that isn't in the game."

After Shinji's outburst, a couple of men who had been talking to Dexter's Uncle turned to look at us.

"Whoa, slow down, Shinji." I put my hands out, motioning him to stop. "We've all had a long week. Why don't you take a few days off, and we'll worry about this when we get back in the office?"

He rubbed the back of his neck and then leaned forward to whisper, "I'm sorry, I know how this must sound…but there are algorithms in the code that weren't there last week. Maybe I didn't notice them until now, but I'm talking about a lot of code, Jack. It all looks like gibberish to me…" Shinji sighed. "I just need someone else to come look at it."

I was a little stunned by the request. Shinji was a better programmer than I was. What did he think I was going to see that he couldn't?

Shinji frowned at my hesitation.

"I know this sounds weird, but I just need to know that I'm not going crazy."

His hands were shaking as he reached up to wipe his brow with a drenched rag. Shinji may have been a little eccentric, but I already knew he wasn't crazy.

"Okay," I said. "Let's go have a look at it."

But as soon as I'd spoken, a strong hand weighed down my shoulder.

"Mr. Valentine, Mr. Takeuchi," David Hayward's voice boomed from behind. "May I have a moment?"

I turned to face him. Meryl was approaching on his heels. Emmerich had already started for the car. We all shook hands and exchanged contrived, quickly forgotten greetings.

"I have been talking with Ms. Silver here about my investment in…"

He paused, searching. He couldn't remember the fucking name of his own son's company.

"Electric Sheep," he snapped a finger. "I have some exciting plans in the works, and I'd like to sit down and talk with you about them. I'll be stopping by the office tomorrow. How does around eleven sound?"

It sounded terrible. Shinji shot me a look. I knew how he felt. The last thing we needed was Dexter's father wandering the office asking a bunch of questions.

"That sounds good Mr. Hayward, but it would work better for me if we scheduled an appointment for next week. Perhaps a lunch meeting."

"Don't be silly. I'm excited to get rolling with this, and I don't want to waste any more time."

"With all due respect, sir, I'd like to put together a technical demonstration for you that will best show what we've been working on, and that might take some–"

"Oh come now! You boys have been working on this thing for nearly a year already, I'm sure you have plenty to show."

He leaned forward and put his hand on my shoulder again. This time he spoke a little softer.

"I need to know what kind of legacy my son left."

The insensitivity in his eyes scared me. But there was something else rolling around behind his eyes as well. His tone suggested there was more to his statement than its literal interpretation.

He turned to walk away, but threw one last remark over his shoulder before he was gone.

"Some exciting things are coming down the pipe, Jack. You'll see."

I turned to Meryl and Shinji; my anger rose sharply. Why couldn't anyone resist talking about business at Dexter's funeral?

"Jack, I'm sorry," Meryl started. "He had a lot of questions about ESP's finances, and we just started going over a few–"

"Damn it Meryl!" I turned up the volume with every word. "Couldn't you pick a worse time to talk about money with our investor than at his only child's funeral?"

"What!"

Meryl's face scrunched in surprise; it unfolded into indignation. She jabbed an acrylic nail into her chest.

"Do you think I have absolutely no couth, Jack? He approached me! He wanted to talk money."

I backed off. I didn't feel sorry at the time, but I opened my mouth to apologize anyway. She held up a hand to stop me. We were all a little emotionally strung out; forgiveness would have to wait.

"Look, I'm used to you being an ass," she said. "Just come to work tomorrow prepared to impress his balls off. I will deal with the rest." She turned to leave. "See you in the morning, Shinji."

She started for her car and, without looking back, she waved, but it looked like she was flipping me off.

I turned to Shinji. Neither of us seemed to be able to speak. Sweating from every pour in his body, he looked physically worn out and psychologically defeated. But, if we both looked how we felt, then Shinji was the healthy one.

CHAPTER TEN: RESTLESS SLEEP

Dexter worked in a world set against him. His vision for Evi must have been a little unclear. Not because he didn't know what he wanted. And not because there has never been a universal definition for artificial intelligence, though there really hasn't. His biggest problem would have been trying to pin down human intelligence. Despite all of humanities forward progress, we've never been able to properly define – or even understand – our own intellect.

Intelligence isn't confined to the human faculty of learning, reasoning, or understanding, because animals are capable of all those things as well. The term can not be defined as the capacity to recall facts or solve problems either, because we've created basic machines that can also do all that. Intelligence has always been a blanket term, encompassing many capacities unique to the human mind. There has always been something immeasurable about the concept. There have always been functions of the mind too abstract to put to words: belief, rationalization, intuition.

Not that any of that has stopped us from trying. The list of pioneers who have tried to create a synthetic thinking machine is practically unending. After my encounter with professor Hojo, I'd done a little research of my own into thinking machines. What I'd discovered made me uneasy.

During the fifties, an MIT computer program received better scores on its calculus exam than most students. During the 1960s and 70s, the University of Edinburgh worked on a computer called Freddy, which was taught to recognize any object placed in front of it. The, in 1964, a language machine was developed that could translate English into Russian and vice versa. A simulation of the human mind appeared just around the corner.

The post-war boom of the 1950s created a mindshare, an unspoken consensus, that humanity's future held unlimited prosperity. The arrival of the computer, with its almost human-like ability to process symbols, allowed society to dream big. After thousands of years of myth, a real man-made intelligence seemed to lie on the tip of tomorrow.

It is no surprise then that humanity's attempts fell short – as they often do – from these lofty expectations. Reality is sadly less impressive than a dream.

Freddy, the visual recognition computer took ten minutes to identify a cup. The MIT computer, which had outscored most students in Math, was little more than a fancy database program, and wasn't capable of composing a single book report or thesis statement. And, in a tragicomic account, the revolutionary translating machine destroyed more than just a sentence's syntax when it translated, "the flesh is willing, but the spirit is weak" into "the vodka's good, but the steak is awful."

Scientists around the world knew about these failures, and they still ran wild with theories. They continued to dream, leaving a legacy of broken science fiction utopias in their wake. Man's reach continually exceeded his grasp.

I tried to describe these problems to a few people at Dexter's funeral, but all I received were odd looks and blank smiles. I decided to leave. Dexter's reception was too claustrophobic anyway. I considered going back to Dexter's empty house. His Last Will and Testament stated that all his possessions would be auctioned off and the proceeds donated to charity, and I wouldn't have many opportunities to go back. But there wasn't anything left for me at Dexter's house.

I went home.

Now that Dexter's body was in the ground, I felt like there was a small amount of finality to his story. This tragedy had deprived me of sleep for days. Now that it was over I was hoping for at least one night's rest. I told myself that after one quiet night on my couch, I'd bounce back. I was lying to myself. My body was begging for the deep embrace of true rest. It was something my couch couldn't provide. It was a tranquility you never got from sleep.

Halfway down the hall from my apartment, I paused. The small figure of a man was curled up at the foot of my door. Like a lost child, his knees were tucked in tight next to his chest. When he saw me approach, he unraveled quickly and scrambling nervously to his feet. He was still dressed in the suit he'd worn to Dexter's funeral. Only now it was heavy with a day's worth of stank.

"Shinji? What are you doing here?"

"Jack."

He clumsily strained the syllable of my name to imply hello. His face looked ragged, weatherworn. I'd lost him somewhere between the gravesite and the reception. I hadn't expected to find him waiting for me at my apartment.

"I've been waiting for you," he said.

Clearly.

"You okay?" I asked.

"Yeah...uh...you know," he shrugged.

Shinji raked to tips of his fingers through oily hair and glanced down both ends of the hall. His mannerisms reminded me of a nervous jackrabbit.

"I think I'm being stalked," he finally admitted.

I shook the hum of exhaustion out of my head. I didn't have time for this. I was on the verge of collapse. In that moment, it seemed like the easiest thing for me to do would have been to lie down on the wooden floor of my hallway and pass out.

"What?" I asked.

"I…I think I'm being watched. I think someone m-might want to murder me."

It took me a minute to process what he was saying. I was fading out of rational thought.

"Someone might want to murder you?"

The words sounded more ridiculous in my mouth.

"Who?" I asked.

Shinji looked over his shoulder again then leaned in close enough to whisper.

"I don't know. It's just this feeling I have…but somebody is definitely following me."

I looked at him for a moment hoping he would disappear. Maybe this was a dream; maybe I was already asleep. Maybe it was just an insomnia hallucination. I leaned against my doorframe for support as I unlocked the door.

"I'm sorry, Jack, I didn't know what to do…I didn't know where to go. But I can't be alone right now."

"Come in," I said as I tossed my keys in a tray by the door.

"Thank you, Jack."

Shinji practically ran into my apartment. He glanced around the room for a minute then sat down on my couch and stared at the black screen of my TV.

"Thanks for giving me a place to stay tonight. I swear it's just for tonight. You'll hardly know I'm here."

I didn't realize that I'd just offered up my apartment as a hotel, but I didn't say anything. I searched for a question that would help me understand what was going on, but I couldn't think straight. I didn't know where to begin.

Shinji didn't seem interested in talking much anyway.

"Can I turn on your TV?" he asked.

I gestured openly, and he started fumbling through my remotes. The screen flicked on, and the late night news started counting down the day's events. Another truck overturned on the highway. The state was proposing an extension to the interstate. Farmers voiced their fears about the summer drought. Overseas a flood had devastated a third-world village. Footage showed a small boy curled up on the roof of his home, crying.

Shinji changed the channel. Beautiful celebrities laughed. God's irony, if He existed, was perpetually evident.

I began to feel the weight of my eyelids. My senses were shutting down. The world was taking on a dreamy haze and my apartment's walls started to move. Out of the corner of my eye, I could see fleeting nonexistent figures.

"It hurts to breath after you drown."

"What was that?" I asked.

Shinji turned to me.

"I didn't say anything."

He turned back to the TV; an ad for a local jewelry store played soft piano music.

I was practically dreaming already. I had a foot it two realities.

"Sorry if I startled you earlier," Shinji said.

"Don't worry about it," I said.

"Is tonight a bad night for you?" he said.

Yes.

"No, don't worry about it," I said.

"You really don't mind if I stay here for one night?" he asked.

"No, don't worry about it," I said.

I felt stupid for saying the same thing three times. I was so tired I'd run out of word.

"I'm exhausted," I added. "I think I'm gonna go crash."

As soon as the words were out of my mouth, I froze. My heart began to race. I hadn't realized what having a houseguest meant to my sleeping habits. Where was I going to sleep? Not in the bedroom. I couldn't go in there.

"Hey uh…why don't you take my bed tonight," I offered. "The sheets are clean."

Shinji stared at me with a wide expression. He looked like I'd just asked him to sleep with my girlfriend. He shook a hand in protest.

"No, no, I can't do that."

He turned quickly back to the television and tried to change the channel but muted the volume instead.

I was beginning to breathe heavily. I couldn't let this happen.

"Seriously, I insist. I want you to be comfortable."

Shinji's expression turned pained, as though it hurt him to turn down my generosity. But he wouldn't look at me. He continued to look at the remote; turning the TV's volume back up and changing the channel.

"No please, Jack. I'll be fine out here. I'm not tired anyway. I'll just watch TV for awhile."

That was it. I didn't have enough fight in me to press further, but I stared at Shinji for a moment longer than I should have before meekly saying, "Okay." I got up and turned to make my descent down a long hall, to a bedroom I hadn't entered in years.

The door handle was cool; I felt hypersensitive to its icy grip. The hair on my legs stood on end from a draft coming through the bottom gap. I turned the knob, and the door creaked open by itself. Thick, musty air smashed into me. I took a step forward.

For a moment, I wondered if Shinji was watching me from behind. Could he see how hesitant I was to enter the room? Could he see the tremble of my hands? Could he smell my fear? I tried not to panic, but I didn't want him to see my anxiety.

I casually turned to close the door. Looking back down the hall I could see that Shinji wasn't even within eyesight. I sighed.

I took in some of the stale air and flicked on the light; it took a moment to flicker on. The room was an eerie sight. For the span of a few deep breaths, I had trouble believing I was standing in a real place, and not somewhere that had always been just a memory – a figment of my nightmares.

Everything looked smaller – less significant – than I had remembered it. The door to the bathroom was on the left. I hadn't seen this side of it for a long while. Even though it looked identical on the other side – the side I always saw in the bathroom – looking at the door from this angle put me on edge. I closed my eyes. I could see the pattern of blood lightly splattered across its frame. Long since washed away, the tiny dots were only visible in my mind.

I took stock of the bed. Where everything else had shriveled with time, the bed seemed to have grown. It stodgily filled any extra space the tiny room might have once had. It was too big for one person. More room than two, or even three, people really needed. I wondered why it had felt cramped all those years before when there had been just two of us. With all this space a person would be lonely.

I couldn't sleep in here; the bed was just too damn big.

After just thirty second in this room, I felt like my body was about to split open. Fear pounded against my chest; it was trying to break free. For two years, love and guilt had hardened inside me like a petrified organ – where my heart should have been sat an emotional cancer.

Suddenly, I didn't feel tired. I wondered if Shinji needed anything. I opened the door and walked back into the fresh air of the living room. He was still watching TV. Bill Cosby performed a silly dance as he got into bed with his wife. A studio audience howled with laughter.

Shinji looked up.

"Sorry, is this too loud?"

"No, don't worry about it."

How many times could I say that?

"I...I was just wondering if you needed anything before I..."

I didn't finish the sentence. Shinji stared.

"Do you want sheets or...anything...else?"

Shinji looked over at the blanket I kept at the end of the couch; the one I used every night.

"I'll be fine," he said. "Thank you."

He looked expectantly at me, and I realized I was just standing there, staring at him.

"Good night," I said.

"Good night," he said.

I made the slow walk back to the bedroom.

I took off the tie and jacket I'd been wearing all day. Then remembered I didn't have a place to put them. My entire wardrobe was in the living room closet; I couldn't go back out there again.

I stared at the bed; my mind raced back through time. Images swam across the sea of my wounded memory. The flash of smoke. The echo that haunts my every silence. Red freckles on white walls. Running forward and holding her in my arms for the last time.

I tried to shake the fragments of that event out of my head, tried to see the bed for what it really was – wood and metal, cotton and plastic. But my wife's memory was soaked into those sheets.

The bed sighed as I sat on it, wheezed again as I laid back uncomfortably. I didn't get under the covers; they were too heavy. Then I surrendered my body to its weariness. A storm was coming. A nightmare. I closed my eyes and embraced it.

0100101001000001010000110100101100100000000100
1100010000001001010010010100101
00110001001100

CHAPTER ELEVEN: JACK & JILL

"It hurts to breath after you drown," she said, tubes coming out of her nose, a needle in her right arm feeding her liquid nutrition from a plastic bag.

I know what she means; I almost drowned once myself. When I was eleven, my grandfather took me sailing. Half a century of experience couldn't save us from the storm in which we were caught. I start to tell her about it, but she didn't need to hear the story. She's heard it a dozen times before.

That morning she'd had another dizzy spell and fainted into her bath water. I was quick to find her, but her lungs took in too much water, and I had to perform CPR. She was weaker then, frail like a porcelain doll. All I could do was sit and keep her company during exhausting trips to the hospital. While she slept, I would hold her tiny hands in mine; they were thin and pale from chemicals that were killing her as they killed the cancer inside her.

I never understood the allure of red hair until I'd met Jill. She had been a sculpted beauty: full lips and tight thighs, placid blue eyes contrasted by slightly toasted skin. She was exotic. But, her allure went far deeper than skin. She was a force of nature: her personality was magnetic – her touch electric. Her passions were as dangerous and intoxicating as fire. She was a woman of extremes, and I couldn't stay away. I didn't want to.

We met in college. One night, eight of us piled into one car and drove to the movies. I rode in the trunk, hoping to impress the girls. I don't know what most of them thought, but I caught the attention of at least one. The only one that mattered.

I knew Jill was special from the beginning. She remembered names, dates, and random details. Not just any name, date, or random detail; she could recall every name, date, and random detail that that was place into her mental filing cabinet with the snap of a finger. She would remember the cashiers name from the grocery store two days later. She knew the release dates for all her favorite films. She made shopping lists entirely in her head, and never forgot a single item. She could recall all her locker combinations from grade school. She called her memory a gift. I lovingly called her a freak.

That made her smile.

She studied movies like a religion. Old detective films, westerns, bad eighties action films. She made me watch animated children's pictures and Chinese kung-fu flicks. Those were her favorites. She knew more about obscure independent and foreign films than I did about video games. She liked popular films as well – movies about gangsters, and sports stars, and everyday heroes.

We got into an argument when we first met about how many James Bond films Sean Connery had made. I was young and prideful, and wasn't going to let a girl show me up. But I was wrong. As payment I took her out to dinner. I was happy to be wrong.

That was our first date.

She took pictures. Professional photographs. She was a struggling artist; trying to make a career out of a hobby. She sold her first photo to a local newspaper when she was sixteen, and got hooked to the idea of selling photos for a living. By the time we met, her pictures were in local coffee shops all over the city. By the time she was diagnosed with cancer, she was getting published in national travel and nature magazines.

Our apartment was her studio. Framed pictures on every wall. Most of them are in boxes now – in a storage shed in North Beach. I kept one. It's a picture of a pod of dolphins. She spotted them one morning during a cruise along Mexico's coast. We were on our honeymoon.

Now the dolphins seem lonely, hanging crooked on one bathroom wall – a reminder that I'm alone.

Jill loved to travel. Three or four times a year she'd be off to somewhere exotic. It cost her a lot to travel so much, so she had few worldly possessions. By the time we were married, she had maxed out four credit cards traveling the world. She didn't care. Her life was filled with memories from all corners of the globe. One semester in London she'd collected sixteen new passport stamps. Eventually she got paid to travel to take photos. Ontario, Venezuela, some remote spot in Alaska's backcountry. She didn't care where she was going. At times, almost randomly, she would pack up and head out, just to see what she could find.

Sometimes I traveled with her. One morning we woke up at four in the morning to hike up a mountain and take pictures of the sunrise. The weather was cold, and the hike took longer than we'd planned, but the clearing we reached was gorgeous. Purple mountains reflected a golden sun onto a valley of blossoming lilacs. I wish she'd taken a picture, but by the time Jill got her equipment set up, clouds had rolled in, making it too dark. She didn't feel like the weather was right for a photo. She'd missed her chance by a matter of minutes. Later we had to hide under a Ponderosa Pine too poorly suited to hold back the abrupt thunderstorm that had sprang up. Jill started to cry, but not because of the rain.

I'd gotten down on one knee and handed her a ring.

Jill was fearless: of spiders, of heights, of scary movies, of new experiences, of pretty much anything. If a friend wanted to try skydiving, and needed moral support, Jill would have held their hand the whole way down. During one trip we took to Iceland, I saw her take a bite of Hákarl – which is something like putrefied shark. This was before our guide had finished describing the cubed meat. As we later learned, the local dish is made from the Basking shark, and contains a lot of uric acid, which is actually poisonous when fresh. It smells like ammonia once it's prepared, but it's edible. Jill gagged after impulsively throwing the mystery fish in her mouth, but she swallowed it like a trooper. She was even willing to go for another round after we'd gotten a drunk on wine and Brennivín.

Jill drooled over cookbooks. She'd read them in bookstores, gaping wide-eyed over the pictures like a teenager looks at pornography. She played the flute in college. She absolutely hated standing in line. She couldn't stand Jazz. She made silly faces when she thought no one was looking, and talked to herself in the shower. She liked to doodle on napkins in restaurants. She had one cigarette whenever she drank. It took her a month to work through a pack of smokes. She had subscriptions to nearly a dozen magazines, mostly for the photos. Her favorite movie was either *Amadeus* or *Beauty and the Beast* depending on the day you asked. Her favorite color: green. Her favorite food: fried rice.

But there was a darker side to Jill.

She suffered through intense bouts of depression. Like the flu, it happened about once a year. There was a season to her mood. Whenever she caught this emotional sickness her work slowed, eventually it stopped. She would sit on the couch and watch movies late into the night – whatever happened to be on at two in the morning. Curled up under a blanket, baggy-eyed, a bowl of ice cream in hand, she even looked diseased.

Jill was the insomniac. I never had trouble sleeping until she passed away. It was her legacy to me.

We had fights. In retrospect, many of them don't make sense. One of our worst started because we couldn't agree on what kind of wine to take to a party. Jill's bipolar emotions were decay on our relationship. Near the end, our whole marriage was something like a tightrope act. We each performed our duties, but there was a real chance that at anytime one of us might lose their grip and fall. Eventually, I slipped, and she fell.

One day, while digging through our closet, I found a pile of letters. They were rejection letters from a publisher for a children's photo book Jill had been working on. I was surprised to find them hidden in our closet. I was even more surprised to learn that Jill was working on a children's book. She'd never told me.

I walked into our living room with the letters. She hadn't been feeling good that week; she was relaxing on the couch with a couple magazines. I didn't even have to open my mouth. As soon as she saw me holding the mail-worn papers, her body went rigid.

"Where did you find those?" she said angrily.

"Behind your shoes. I was looking for my black belt."

She just looked at me.

"Jill? What is all this?" I asked.

"You were going through my stuff?"

Her voice squealed like the wheels of a breaking train and she jumped forward to snatch the crinkled sheets from my hand.

"Your stuff?"

I was momentarily stunned.

"...I was looking through *our* things." I added the word, "honey," but the pitch of my voice disfigured the gentleness of the word.

"You've been working on a book?" I asked.

"It's just..."

Frustrated, she tossed the papers on the coffee table, then looked embarrassingly at her feet.

"...it's just a silly side project."

"Why didn't you ever say anything?"

"..."

"Jill?"

She shook her head. She didn't know what to say.

"Hey, I think it's a great idea. But was there a reason you needed to hide it?"

She looked down at the letters, and picked them back up. She didn't seem to know what to do with them. She was on the verge of tears – an unstable nuclear reactor.

I tried to take the pages away from her. We grappled for a second, and I ended up with a few corners in my hand. Most of the pages ended up on the floor.

"Why do you always do this to yourself?" I said frustrated. "Do you enjoy torturing yourself?"

"You know what, Jack," she bit back. "You tell me that I shouldn't feel like shit all the time, doesn't help."

I threw up my hands.

"Fine! I give up. It's not my problem that you kept the letters. I really don't care if you want to fixate on your rejections."

I threw the shreds in my hand to the ground.

"But why on earth did you feel the need to keep them hidden like some kind of secret passion?"

"I don't know…"

I didn't know what to do with that. All I knew at the time was that I was really upset. She'd kept something hidden from me, something absurd. I felt like I'd just caught her having an affair. My stomach turned sick.

"What else are you hiding from me?"

"Nothing."

What was I hiding from her? I could feel my rage building. I couldn't stop myself.

"You know what, Jill. I'm sick of you moping around the house complaining all day. You're not doing anything productive, and you're not taking very good care of yourself. You're sick, and you need help!"

She collapsed onto the couch in tears.

"Jack listen, I tried to talk to you. I wanted to tell you about the book. I just…I was scared."

She took heavy breaths, trying to stop the sobbing. I clenched my fist, embraced the anger for fear of my own tears.

"Scared! Of what?"

Of me. Of what I thought of her. I never loved her enough when she was alive. But she couldn't put that into words.

So she said nothing.

"Why does this always happen?" I yelled. "I tell you one thing, and you don't believe me. You don't trust me enough to tell me what you're thinking. We try to talk and you clam up. I don't want to play this game with you anymore."

Her face crumpled, and under a quivering lip she spoke.

"This is a relationship, Jack. Not a game."

But I felt like ours was.

I stormed out of the room like a spoiled child. I was being an idiot, and I was embarrassed. I didn't even know what we were fighting about anymore.

Almost an hour later, Jill came into the bedroom looking repentant.

"I threw them all away," she said.

I looked up. She was standing in the doorframe. I tried to smile — tried to tell her it was okay. I was stupid, and we'd just had a stupid fight, and I didn't mean any of it. But you can't say some of that stuff without opening your mouth.

"I don't know what I'm doing," she said. "I'm tired all the time. I know that I should go out and work. I know that I should try to take some pictures, but it requires so much effort. Most of the time, I don't have a desire for anything."

She approached cautiously, like a puppy who had just been disciplined.

"I know that I should eat, but I don't want to eat. I know that I should run errands, that I should shower, that I should go work out, that I should get out of bed in the morning, but I just can't force myself to do any of it. I just can't force myself to do most of the things I know I should."

She moved past the foot of the bed. She was within reach. I could have stretched out my arms and grabbed her.

"Sometimes my life feels completely wrong. My house feels wrong. My daily routine feels wrong. This shirt I'm wearing feels wrong. I feel like a false person, Jack. Everything about me is wrong. Does that make any sense to you?"

I wanted to tell her that I felt that way all the time, but I didn't.

"I kept something from you, and that was wrong," she said. "I know. I'm sorry. You don't keep secrets in a marriage."

I warmed to that apology about as quickly, or effortlessly, as churning butter. I'd heard it before. Her life was full of emptiness, and mine was too full of empty things. At the time I couldn't sympathize with her. It wouldn't be until after her death that I started dancing with the demons she'd been partnered with for so long.

I pulled her to my side, and we hugged.

"I'm sorry, Jack. So, so sorry."

My shoulder was warm and wet with her tears. I held her for a long while, and then we made love.

Later that night she hacked up black tar. It was cancer.

Jill was a social smoker, so we never really believed the jokes she made about how cigarettes would kill her. We were right to joke. Cigarettes couldn't kill her; Jill survived the cancer. But, she wasn't the same afterwards.

Most people recover from cancer with a new zest for life. Not my Jill. She walked out of the hospital missing some part of herself – mostly her laughter and her smile. Her episodes of listlessness lasted longer. Her bout with depression was a losing battle. She caught her special flu and never recovered.

During chemo, she once told me that the chemicals took away her sense of taste. Everything had a different flavor to it after the treatments. But cancer took away her taste for life. I couldn't pull her back out of the pit she fell in; she'd sunk out of reach.

That was Jill. That was my wife. The woman I had once cared for more than the breath inside my lungs. The other half of my fairytale. My soul mate. My dearly departed. The only woman I've ever truly loved.

And the only woman I've ever killed.

CHAPTER TWELVE: ROUND ONE, ACUISITION

I stared down the barrel of a gun. Like a shark in dark water, the figure had exploded out of the shadows and pointed two revolvers at me. With less than second to react, I let my epileptic trigger finger squeeze off a few shots, and my onscreen enemy folded backwards.

"What the hell's going on in here?"

I turned to see Gordon's head shoved through my office doorway. His mouth swung wide as he surveyed the scene.

"Research."

I pointed to the video capture equipment next to my TV. I had discovered long ago that showing my team tapes of other games was more effective than trying to describe what I wanted them to do. Playing other games was a useful tool for game development. Except that morning I hadn't recorded a single video, and Gordon could clearly see that the recording equipment wasn't on. I had plenty of other work to do; I was just wasting time.

"Meryl said you were in here," Gordon said in a tone that suggested he was skeptical.

"Well, here I am."

Apparently satisfied, Gordon entered my office.

"She also said you were working," he said with a smile so wide I wanted to punch him.

I clenched my teeth.

I don't know why Gordon was at the office that day. It was the day after Dexter's funeral, and several staffers had taken the day off. We were running on a skelton crew. I had come in early to prepare for Michael Hayward's visit, but it hadn't been a productive morning.

"Is this *Tomb Raider*?" Gordon asked.

I nodded. The game had caught Dexter's eye at the Consumer Electronics Show a year or so back, and I'd always meant to play it, but I hadn't found the time. For some reason, that morning it leapt out at me from my game shelf. I was looking for any excuse not to work.

"Looks good," Gordon grunted.

Onscreen my character danced through bullets as my aggressor pressed his attack. I couldn't spare the concentration needed for a conversation.

My digital counterpart was an athletic female archeologist named Lara Croft – a combat gymnast. Together we performed physics-defying acrobatics. These digital catacombs were our stage, and I directed Lara in a ballet of bloodshed. A killer performance where she was the only actor left to bow as the curtain fell.

I was a good choreographer, and Lara was good at taking directions.

My reward for being such a skilled director was to have this power taken away from me. An animated cut scene interrupted my game, wrestling the story back onto prescripted rails. It was a reminder that I was not the architect of this show. I was a player. Less than that. I had been relegated to viewer.

"Well you have my total attention now," Lara said pointing her gun at a down opponent. "I'm not sure if I've got yours though. Hello?"

Our defeated assailant sat a Lara's feet. She wanted to press him for information. I wanted her to pull the trigger. But she wasn't taking directions from me anymore.

There was a time when I had enjoyed scenes like this. I thought they made games more cinematic – made them more mature. Over time, I realized my ignorance. The art of good gaming isn't found in emulating other mediums. That would be a back-step in the evolution of the form. The real substance of a video game is its interactivity.

Humanity loves to interact with its entertainment. We are social creatures; it's in our genetics. For centuries, our primary source of entertainment was telling interactive stories around a campfire. During the height of classical theater, audience participation was encouraged. People rarely watch TV linearly. Viewers flick through stations compulsively, creating their own shows that are part sitcom, part football game, and part news program all within the span of a single timeslot.

People respond to interactivity. It's why games can achieve a level of intimacy with their audience that other art forms lack. It's also why, when developers remove that interactivity – when they pare games back to pure cinematic sequences – they neuter the one element of a game that defines it.

I spun around in my chair and started picking at the remnants of some leftover lo mein that I'd had for breakfast.

Gordon was transfixed by the game.

"This is some impressive tech," he said.

I shrugged wiping away a splash of sauce from a rice noodle that had whipped across my cheek.

Behind me the scene played out.

Lara's assailant, a man with a bloody arm and a terrible Texas accent, spoke about the whereabouts of an ancient artifact and the man who'd taken it.

"Hah, you ain't fast enough for him."

"So you think all this talking is just holding me up?" Lara asked.

"I don't know where his little jackrabbit frog legs are running him to."

I shook my head while stabbing at a piece of chicken with my hashi.

"This is cheesy," I said.

"Yeah," Gordon said snapping out of his transfixed stare. "But I always appreciate the creative strides taken to make the absurd sound clever."

"Reality rarely functions in amusing metaphor," I said grumpily.

"Yeah, but then again, entertainment isn't reality."

It was a good point.

"Whatever," I shrugged.

I turned off the game and hit the switch for the recording equipment before I remember that it wasn't on.

"Kind of dark in here," Gordon said as if he'd just noticed. "What are you, a troglodyte?"

He turned on the lights, and I winced like a vampire under their power.

"Morning, sunshine," he added perkily.

"Gordon, why are you here?"

"Remember when you asked me about that art Dexter wanted for Shrine?"

"Yeah."

I frowned. I felt sick. Exhaustion had me in a death grip. It was the morning after my first real night of sleep in almost a week. My body hadn't wanted to get up that morning. Now that it had tasted sleep, it wasn't going to forgive me for the punishment I'd put it through. Some art request Dexter had made weeks ago didn't seem relevant anymore. All I wanted to do was stay in my office with the shades drawn and stare at the walls.

Fortunately, I have a habit of not doing what I want.

"Do you still want to see it?" Gordon asked.

"Yeah," I grumbled.

I forced my body erect, and followed Gordon out the door and down the hall.

In the art department's bullpen, I leaned over a row of monitors that lined the top of Gordon's desk. The average gaming industry employee probably has half a dozen toys on their desk. Gordon made up for those of us who didn't. He was the poster child for geek, with every action figure from Voltron to Spawn to Dr. Who blanketing his work area. One absurdly expensive Robbie the Robot figurine held a place of honor in front of Gordon's three monitors.

Beside his desk stood a bookshelf filled with art resource books – a range that varied from human anatomy to children's picture books to books of classic and historical architecture. A mini-fridge, well-stocked with frozen pizzas and Mountain Dew sat within impulsive reach. From a framed movie poster, a chainsaw-handed Bruce Campbell surveyed Gordon's entire domain.

Gordon cracked his knuckles before sitting down to pull up the files.

"Okay, this is the Shrine art Dexter wanted."

Gordon's monitor slowly put together a very ornate marble fountain. A stone figure of Galatea bathed in the center of a large basin.

"The texture resolution is too high, and the poly count is too big. Basically we felt that this fountain was too expensive, so we changed it," Gordon finished.

In virtual modeling, all objects (statues, buildings, people, etc.) are built out of simple geometric polygons. Simple math. But even the fastest computer processors in the world have limits to how many simple mathematical shapes they can process at any given time. Therefore, in a game, we set a limited polygon count. We call this maximum processing limit our "budget," and it's something we have to stay under in order to keep the game running at a playable speed.

An alarm went off inside my head. I had been thinking about Pygmalion since Dexter's funeral, but I hadn't been able to figure out what it meant. Something about his reference still nagged me.

"A couple days ago, you said this was from the Pygmalion myth."

"Yeah?" Gordon said raising an eyebrow.

"So, Pygmalion and this goddess were lovers?"

Gordon tilted his head to the side. My understanding of Greek myth gave him genuine pause.

"You could say that."

I hesitated.

"Did she kill him or something?"

I should have stopped guessing. That would have hid my ignorance.

"Well, first of all, Galatea wasn't a goddess. Why does everyone keep saying she was a goddess? She was a statue."

"Uh huh," I said in a counterfeit tone of recollection.

"If I recall correctly," Gordon started, "Pygie made the most beautiful sculpture of a woman anyone had ever seen. She was hot. Imagine Ava Gardner to the power of Farrah Fawcet."

"Okay, let me guess, he fell in love his own work?"

"Hey, you know your mythical tropes."

Gordon nodded as he bent down and opened the mini fridge. He tossed me a can of soda, then cracked one open for himself.

"Hey, I'm not going to judge him," Gordon continued. "He was probably a lonely guy. Maybe he still lived in his mother's basement. Anyway, the gods saw that he was in love with his own creation, and they felt bad for the guy, so they decide to do the whole Pinocchio thing."

"They make her a real boy," I added.

"Right. A real girl anyway. Think of the whole story as a kind of freaky Grecian *Frankenstein*, except with sexual undertones, and nude wrestling." Gordon gulped down half a can of soda. "Anyway, I can pull up the current version of the statue, so you can see the changes. I cut the polys in half and–"

"Hold on."

I grabbed his shoulder then pointed at the fountain's base, which sat suspended in otherwise empty space.

"Is that a plaque on the base of the statue?"

Gordon looked it over.

"Looks like it."

"I think something is written on it. Can you zoom in?"

"Ahh, designers…" Gordon said shaking his head with mock disapproval. "You either overlook the fine details, or obsess about them."

Gordon rotated the model to give us a better viewing angle and then zoomed in on the plaque.

It read:

> Behold True Beauty, Cast In Stone
> Sparked Real Love, Caused Much Upheaval
> Drove Men To Kill And Gods To Moan
> This Water Of Galetea's Evi

"What is this? Some kind of Warren Robinett?" Gordon asked.

Gordon was referencing an Easter egg from an Atari 2600 game called Adventure. In the early days of video game development, programmers didn't receive credit for their work. In 1979, a programmer named Warren Robinett got fed up with this and hid his name inside a secret area within a game called Adventure. He expected that no one would ever find it. Of course, hundreds had.

"This isn't an Easter egg, Gordon. It's a message."

"To who?"

"To me."

Gorgon raised an eyebrow.

"Well, the rhyming schemes off and he forgot to put the 'l' in evil."

"No, he meant to say Evi."

A thrill ran through my chest.

"Are you sure? What's an evi?"

"'This Water Of Galetea's Evi,'" I said, reflecting on the poem. "Evi is in here."

I tapped the screen excitedly. Gordon's must have thought I'd cracked.

"Evi was Dexter's Galatea, and he hid it inside our game," I said.

I starred at Gordon with wild-eyed amazement as it all unraveled. He had no idea what I was talking about. I ran my fingers through my hair.

"God. Shinji's anomalies," I exclaimed finally putting puzzle pieces together that I'd been staring at for days.

Dexter had implanted a copy of the Evi program inside our game. It explained all the problems Shinji was running into. I was so dense not to realize it before, but had Dexter expected me to find it?

I needed to talk with Shinji right away. I didn't even say "bye" to Gordon as I sprinted across the bullpen towards Shinji's cubicle.

Someone shouted my name as I ran, but I ignored it.

"Dexter was a genius," I said breaking into Shinji's cubicle.

Shinji slowing turned to face his intruder.

"I mean, he was an idiot for killing himself, but he was a programming genius," I started to ramble. "Remember that mysterious code you said looked like gibberish – the AI bots that have been doing weird things all week?"

I was talking too fast.

"Yes," Shinji said adjusting his glasses.

"Have you isolated it?"

"Yeah, but that was never the pro–"

"It was Dexter," I blurted.

"Jack," said a quick-tempered female voice running up behind me.

I ignored it for a moment.

"Dexter put that code in there. I need to see it."

Shinji started to fumble around his desk.

"Okay, I can–"

"Jack!"

I looked over my shoulder to see Meryl's frown poking into the cubicle.

"Jack, we need you up front," she said.

"In a minute, we're in the middle of something."

"Jack, now!"

I'd never seen Meryl so anxious.

"Mr. Hayward's assistant is here."

I stared at Meryl for a second then turn to Shinji.

"Pull it up, I want to see it when I get back."

I turned and followed Meryl's heels to the front lobby. I was still a little dazed by my discovery, but I could tell by her manner that something was wrong. When we got to the front door, Emmerich was busy dictating orders to four burly men in mover's uniforms.

"Take everything that's plugged in," he said.

My breath smelled like soy sauce. I was sure my hair was a mess. And I hadn't had time to change into a dress shirt; I was still wearing a paint-stained hoodie I'd thrown on after my brief morning shower. This was not the impression I wanted to give David Hayward's right hand. Nonetheless, I approached Emmerich with as much professional confidence as I could muster.

"Mr. Emmerich, we weren't really expecting you for another hour–"

I paused as the movers breezed past, shuffling deeper into our office.

"What's going on?"

Emmerich grabbed my hand and shook it. His mouth twitched into a cocky half-smile.

"Jack, you doing okay buddy? You look like you woke up on the wrong side of bed this morning."

I had woken up in the wrong bed that morning.

I frowned. "Why are there movers in my office?"

"Yeah, about that…"

Emmerich's casual tone belied his malicious intent, though he didn't hide that for long.

"Mr. Hayward has decided to close down the studio until he has time to review its assets. He apologizes for not coming himself. Unfortunately, he got caught up in some last minute business."

"I'm sorry?" I said numbly. "You said 'close down the studio?'"

Meryl stood behind me, arms crossed, two glaring eyes fixed on Emmerich. One foot tapped maliciously against the carpet. She was waiting to see what I'd do. She must have already had this conversation with Emmerich.

"With Dexter's passing, all his stocks have been inherited by his father. D.B. Hayward Networks is now the primary shareholder of Electronic Sheep. The business will be audited, and its economic viability must be reviewed…"

I closed my eyes and shook my head. He was talking to fast.

"Wait a minute; I don't think Mr. Hayward can–"

"Actually, he can," Emmerich said, stopping my in my tracks.

Emmerich reached into his briefcase, and with the speed of a machine, withdrew a large folder.

"David would like you to review your original contracts if you have any questions. He also wanted to remind you that you signed documents stating that if Electric Sheep Inc. did not achieve a projected profit performance…"

He spoke as though he was reading from an invisible legal document floating in front of his eyes. I tried to listen to the words and failed. If I did understand any of what he was saying it was immediately forgotten. I was vaguely aware of what the original contracts said, and I thought I remembered something about profit performance and corporate buyouts, but at the time it had all seemed like legal filler – the kinds of standard clauses those types of contracts automatically had. I'd taken the business relationship with David Hayward for granted, because he was my best friend's father. Surely, he wouldn't screw us over.

"… in your last two fiscal years, and thereby must make up the loss with sales of corporate stock," Emmerich finished. "Mr. Valentine, Electric Sheep Inc. is now a property of D.B. Hayward Networks LLC. Deal with it."

"Hey, I said you can't take that!"

Gordon came barreling out from the bullpen following two movers whose arms were overflowing with computer equipment.

"Jack, they're taking our computers," Gordon said as if I had somehow failed to notice the two men walking past me.

Meryl looked at me expectantly. What did she want me to do? What could I do?

"What's going on?" Gordon asked staring into my dumbfounded expression.

Emmerich answered for me.

"I'm afraid Electric Sheep will be going through some structural changes, Mr. Freeman."

His talent for remembering names really was impressive.

Emmerich pointed to the folder in my hand.

"Employee compensation, during the interim, is detailed inside. You will find that everyone is well taken care of."

He smiled. I had never seen him look so evil.

I stared at the weight in my hand. It seemed heavy for such a tiny object.

"If you would like to meet with David to talk about the future of the company, call me later in the week and we can set up an appointment?"

I nodded distantly.

Emmerich started for the elevators with the movers.

"Wait a minute," I said.

I chased after him, squeezing onto the elevator before it closed.

"You can't do this."

Emmerich pushed the button for the ground floor.

"Well Jack, I'm not doing it. David is."

"But…I mean…Mr. Hayward can't do this."

He casually opened his PDA and started making notes.

"Jack, I believe I've already explained why he can, and is, doing this."

I tried to think of some argument that would make this all go away. One of the movers sneezed. An elderly couple boarded the elevator on the fifth floor. I fumed, but remained quiet until we reached street level.

"Maybe David should see the demo we've been preparing before he makes any rash decisions," I pleaded on the way out of the building.

"Jack please, act like a grown man. It's already done."

Hundreds of obscenities and insults fluttered trough the hive of my mind. My problem would be picking the best one to start with. The world was spinning around me.

The two movers we'd come down with were already loading their truck.

Emmerich touched a button on his keys and his car beeped to life. I looked the vehicle over. It was familiar. Once my eyes rested on the license plate, I realized why.

"Nice car." My voice cracked with anger, excitement, and fear.

"Yeah, it gets me around," he said smugly.

"Use it for all your errands?"

"If you really like it, Jack, maybe someday I'll let you take it for a test drive."

"Do you steal all your computers with it?"

I pointed at the back of the BMW, to a license plate that had been smashed into my memory by a computer monitor. The first three letters were MGS.

Emmerich's look of shock lasted only a millisecond, but it was enough. He tilted his head back and put on a confused look.

"Thanks for this, by the way." I pointed to the soft gash on my forehead. "I guess I can return the favor now."

"I don't know what you're talking about," Emmerich said opening his car door.

"Don't play dumb. You stole Dexter's PC. Why? And why is Mr. Hayward really shutting us down?"

Emmerich looked me over then leaned in close. He placed his hand on my shoulder. Surprisingly, it didn't burn like a demon. His tone was as close to friendly as he could muster.

"You really should be taking better care of yourself," he said. "Get some rest, and think this through before you do anything that gets you hurt."

Then he threw on his driving glasses and practically jumped into his car.

"I have another meeting to get to, but call me if there is any trouble moving the equipment."

"Fuck you," I said.

But he was already halfway down the block.

CHAPTER THIRTEEN: INDICISION

"How about Thai?" I said flipping through the takeout menus I usually kept magnetized to my fridge.

"Thai is fine. What happened to Chinese?" Shinji said humped over my PC, feverishly hacking away at the keys.

"I like Chinese," I said. "I'm just trying to keep my options open."

Thirty seconds after Emmerich gave me the business finger and drove off, I'd burst into the ESP bullpen, whispered something to Gordon about stalling the movers, and made a beeline for Shinji's desk. I told him to back up every line of code, and then we smuggled Evi out of the building.

Five hours later the ESP offices were cleaned out.

Shinji and I headed back to my place to explore Dexter's secret AI.

The program was a mess. There were too many lines of code, it was impossible for any person to follow the logic. In many cases there was no complete logic circle. It was as if the program circled back on itself, creating redundant patterns, which would have cause any normal program to freeze or crash. Eventually we got tired of staring at programming language and Shinji decided to try and run the thing on my wimpy PC. I decided to order us lunch. Neither of us had been successful.

"Here's a sandwich place that delivers."

I flashed the menu at Shinji who grunted an, "okay" without even looking at it.

"What happened to Chinese?" he asked again.

I kept digging. Nothing sounded good.

"Maybe we should just order a pizza," I said.

"Pizza's fine. Let's do that."

"I don't know. Maybe I don't want pizza. How do you feel about Indian?"

"What happened to Chinese?"

"All right," I gave up. "I'll order Chinese."

I walked over to the phone then snapped my fingers.

"Although that burrito place across the street is really good, and we wouldn't have to wait. I could just walk over there."

"Jack," Shinji stopped and looked over. "I don't care anymore. Just get me something to stick in my mouth."

I picked up the phone and placed an order for sesame chicken, beef and broccoli, and a large order of fried rice.

I've come to realize that my persona is really made up of three different people. One is the careless, bumbling Jack of the past. That version of me really has no clue what I want; he's always making decisions and choices that I don't like. Then there is future Jack. He's the unfortunate inheritor of a life he won't like, a life he wouldn't have chosen for himself. Finally there is the Jack that is stuck between the two. Present me. A me who cluelessly tries to shape the mistakes of his past into a life that he thinks will please future Jack, while at the same time assuredly looking back at efforts of past Jack and wondering – with a frown – why he even bothered. It's not that the three parts of myself are incompetent. I'm not impossible to please. It's just that my dissociative personality schisms have three wildly different views of what pleases Jack.

I don't know what I want from life. I don't even know what I want for lunch.

"All right, it's working," Shinji said.

I ran over to the computer and looked over his shoulder. The Shrine level sat onscreen. Shinji moved over and let me sit down. I started to explore the pixilated stone roads and blocky Greek architecture we'd built for our game. This was it; I was finally going to get another chance to talk with Evi.

I wandered that level for half an hour without seeing anything. The world was hollow.

"This version includes Dexter's extra coding?" I asked

Shinji patiently hovered over my shoulder.

"Yes."

"There's nothing here," I said. "Where are the bots?"

Shinji shrugged.

I didn't really know what I had expected. I guess I had hoped I would turn on the computer and Evi would be standing there, or sitting there, or whatever you wanted to call it. I guess I'd expected to be able to talk with it again, but I didn't know how to call up the prompts I'd seen in Dexter's home.

"Try the palisades," Shinji suggested. "They hang out there a lot."

I took his advice and began moving towards the high fenced in area.

"What happened last time you saw them?" I asked.

Shinji took a moment.

"Hmm, it's hard to describe. They were just sort of milling about, like bees in a hive."

And now they were gone.

"Jack?" Shinji asked timidly.

"Yeah?"

"What was Dexter doing?"

I stared at the still screen.

"He was trying to create a new kind of game AI, something smarter than the usual architecture."

"Something more human?" he asked.

"Yeah, something like that."

Shinji thought about this for awhile.

"Kind of pointless, don't you think?" he asked.

"Pointless? Why?"

"Video games are an illusion. We don't create programs to be intelligent; we create programs to simulate intelligence."

"Yeah," I hesitated. "But if you had a program that really was intelligent, the experience would be more exciting."

"Except it wouldn't. That's why it's an illusion. We don't program game AI to beat us, because it would every time if we did. A computer knows the perfect line to run in a race, but we tell it not to take that line. A computer program could have a perfect aim, but we make our AI bots shoot wildly. If computers were truly intelligent, it wouldn't be a fair fight. They'd win every time."

"Okay," I countered. "But if a player feels like his opponent is dumb it's not fun either. You have to make people feel like they've overcome a challenge. You have to make them believe that their opponent knows what its doing. People like facing off against real human opponents, because they poise a real challenge."

"Real people aren't computers. Computers are faster and more adept with a game's rules than people will ever be. That's why we set up algorithm to perform scripted situations for various events. We dumb the computer down."

"I don't know Shinji, maybe you're just being pessimistic. Who knows how future programming will work. Maybe we won't have to fake it anymore. Fifteen years ago game AI was a few trivial lines of code; did you ever expect that we'd get to where we are now?"

Shinji frowned.

"Fifteen years ago a whole program was a few trivial lines of code. I used to write entire games where the code could be published within a few pages of a magazine for others to retype into their computers. When you're programming on a 640k DOS machine, all you can really do is write a bunch of positive 'if this/then that' rules, but we still had to be careful not to write programs where the machine won every time.

We've always been trying to simulate intelligence, not create it."

"Are you saying that Dexter wasn't developing this for a game?" I asked.

"I don't know what he was doing, but there is a big difference between writing a code that plays chess, writing a code that can run through a maze, and a writing code that simulates a conversation. I don't even think they should share the same term. AI is too broad a description. If a computer knows how to beat you, and it's programmed to beat you, it will beat you."

I thought about that for a bit. Shinji may have been smarter than me, but that didn't mean he was right.

"Dexter always said that the best thing a game can do is deliver an exciting experience with invisible technology," I said. "Maybe that's what this program was supposed to do. What you're describing sounds like a bunch of energetic killbots, and you're right, if we created a bunch of them, no one would have any fun. But if your opponent was a program that seemed intelligent, so intelligent it made human-like decisions – even human-like mistakes – well I don't think there's anything more exciting than that. That must have been what Dexter was trying to do with Evi. It doesn't sound pointless to me."

Shinji leaned back in shock. I smiled.

"I think it wants you to follow," he said.

"What?"

He pointed to the computer monitor. I turned to see a shadowy figure at the edge of the level. It stood barely visible behind a wooden fence. Through the slits I could feel it staring me down.

My monitor went black.

Even though the evening sun was splashing through my windows, a midnight shiver crawled through me. It was the sensation of being in the same room with a ghost that I'd experience at Dexter's the day after he died.

Shinji and I stared at one another.

"Input username," popped onscreen.

Shinji didn't seem surprised or agitated. I realized that he must have seen this part of the program too.

I typed, "Jack."

The screen flashed, and we were suddenly standing outside the digital reconstruction of my apartment. I glanced at Shinji. Nothing seemed to surprise him. I made my way up to the fourth floor of the building and stood in front of my door. I waited. Did I really want to enter? How much of this was I ready to show Shinji?

As I reached out to touch the door of my virtual apartment, a knock came against the wood of my actual apartment door.

My stomach spun. Shinji and I looked at each other and waited.

There came another knock.

Shinji got up and padded slowly to answer it. As I heard him open my front door, the door onscreen swung wide.

I could see a digital version of myself hunched over a small grey box representing my PC. I took a deep breath. I was afraid to turn around and see what Shinji was looking at.

"The Chinese is here," Shinji called out behind me.

But I was too busy staring at my doppelganger, as he turned around and looked me over.

Behind me, I could her Shinji paying for the food.

I dialogue box blinked onscreen. A question appeared inside.

"What do you know about guns?"

I didn't know how to answer, so I stared at the screen.

Shinji closed the door and out of the corner of my eye I could see him take the food into the kitchen.

"Anything happen yet?" he asked.

I never looked up from the monitor. I could feel a bead of sweat working its way around my temple.

"What do you know about guns?" the message came again.

I knew a lot about guns. I knew that Samuel Colt – wildly popular as the man who invented the revolver – had filed for a patent on the revolving handgun in August of 1839. I knew that before Samuel Colt, hunting and killing was done with flint-loaded rifles. Built for speed and multiple shots, the revolver made guns an intimate device of death.

"It won't happen again," came another message.

"I know," I typed.

"But you think it will. What do you know about guns?"

I know that while a gun holds far less value than gold, it steals something far more precious. I know that such a small construction of metal can inflate a man's confidence. I know that guns can open mouths money can't grease. I know they awaken sleeping children, make mothers cry, and drive grown men to beg. I know one gun can ruin a family. One hundred can transform a group of thugs into street kings. And one million can reshape a nation. I knew a lot about guns. I didn't like them.

My digital self stood and walked forward. Suddenly I was aware of another person in the room with us. A digital version of Claire stood docilely in the corner.

"What do you know about guns?"

"A lot," I typed.

"Where do you keep yours?"

"In a safe place."

I have a gun. It's still hidden in my empty sock drawer. It's only been used once.

"You're worried about it."

"Yes."

"And you're worried about her."

My vision flitted between the digital pictures of Claire and myself.

"Yes."

"You'll end it, because you think you have to."

I adjusted in my seat uneasily.

"Do you have anything to drink?" Shinji called out from the kitchen.

"Uh…" I muttered; I was too focused on the screen in front of me.

I heard Shinji in the other room, rooting through the fridge.

The dialogue box spat out one last line of text.

"You'll end it, because you think you have to save her."

My doppelganger held up his knife and shifted his attention to Claire. He moved towards her. She backed away in fear, and became pinned against the wall. These tiny people were ugly, angular renditions, but there was something creepily human about their movement.

I stared at the screen so closely – so intently – that I fell in.

With a click everything became hyper real. There was no computer world. No real world. There was just me. And Claire. Alone in a room. My five senses were on steroids. I could smell her fear, taste her sweat. The air around me was electric energy. It rubbed uncomfortably against my body.

With a spasm, the muscles along my arm jerked up. Then I was staring down the length of my forearm. I was looking at the bloody hump of a handle I'd just buried inside her chest. Without warning, invisible needles shot through my hand, and I twisted the blade. Her whimper was a tiny thing, but it crashed against me like a nuclear explosion. Her chest erupted into a showerhead. Her digital DNA washed over me.

Oh God! What had I done? I wanted to scream, but where my lungs should have been sat an empty space. I moved to hold her, but she fell too fast. Tears trailed behind like frozen diamonds. Floorboards clapped like thunder as she landed.

Then – with the inhalation of a single deep breath – reality snapped back. The screen went black again.

"What happened?"

Shinji stood behind me stuffing rice into his mouth and staring at the blank monitor. When he looked at me, he had to mask a small amount of shock.

"Are you okay?" he asked. "You look pale."

Sweat flicked from my eyebrows as I tried to catch my breath. I looked at Shinji then down the hall to the closed bedroom that hid dark memories. I should have never gone back in there; I'd let something terrible loose.

"We're—"

My voice cracked, and I pushed large wet lumps down my throat.

"We need to go talk to a professor."

CHAPTER FOURTEEN: THE GOLDEN SEA

"A strip club?" Shinji said as we pulled into the parking lot of a yellow stained building. "This is where we're meeting this professor?"

The sign on the roof read: The Golden Saucer – A Premier Gentleman's Club. I was surprised myself. I hadn't heard of The Golden Saucer until I'd called up Professor Hojo. Even then, he'd made it sound like a bar.

After the events with the movers, I knew that I'd eventually have to confront Mr. Hayward. He'd sent his assistant to break into his son's home, and then seized all of ESP's computers. Somehow he must have known about Evi, but I needed more information about the program before I confronted one of California's most powerful men.

The club's fridge-shaped bouncer welcomed us in with a gracious smile. A female bartender with spunky hair and dark makeup served a few drunks lining the bar, but most of the scattered tables were unoccupied. Only one of the three stages was in use. The whole remained as dark as an underground garage despite the hundreds of Christmas lights dangling from the walls. This place was a dive.

"You know," Shinji said, "You can tell a lot about a guy based on where he sits in a place like this."

"How so?"

"Well if he sits up front, by the stage, he's interested in the women."

"We're in a strip club, Shinji. Everyone is interesting in the women."

"You mean not everyone is here for a covert meeting about secret AI projects?" Shinji said with perfect comedic speed.

I probably would have laughed, but I was so surprised he'd even made a joke that I didn't know how to react. I was beginning to realize that I knew very little about my lead programmer.

"If you sit by the stage, your main focus is the girls," Shinji continued. "You come here to stimulate fantasies. If you sit at the bar, you're more interested in the alcohol. You have sorrows to drown."

Shinji pointed at me as though I was one of these hypothetical people.

"That's why it's darker by the bar. That makes it easier to hide," Shinji added. "Then there are the coasters. The guys who used to come here because it was fun, but life changed on them. These guys used to sit at the bar or the stage. They lived it up with drinks and dances, but then something terrible happened. Slowly the comfort of this place wore itself thin. Now they just come here because they don't know what else to do."

Shinji pointed to a man in the darkest corner of the club.

"That kind of guy," he finished.

It was the Professor. He was sitting alone, far from the stage, but not too far from the bar. His head hung as he gazed into an empty glass.

We approached him.

"Professor Hironobu Hojo?" I asked.

Hiro looked up defensively.

"Remember me? Jack, from the other day."

Hiro gave a vague nod then stared down his drink. Shinji and I pulled up a couple chairs. A cocktail waitress approached to take our order. She wore an outfit that may have come from a Victoria's Secret catalogue. In fact, she looked like she could have walked out of one. She was just a cocktail waitress, but she was healthier than any of the girls onstage. The dancers looked like they had been ridden harder than a champion racehorse.

As the waitress left, Hiro's eyes spun after her. His head towed along for the ride.

A hunger inside me stirred, but I stuffed it back down.

"In this place, love's on sale," Hiro said. "If you need it."

"Who doesn't," I wanted to say.

Instead I looked over at Shinji. He looked oddly comfortable in this place.

"Thanks for meeting with us," I said turning back to Hiro. "I was hoping you could answer a few more questions we had about Evi."

"Mr. Valentine," Hiro said. "I feel like I should tell you a story I heard as a child."

Hiro looked in my direction, but not at me. He was dazed, lost even, a man not completely in the moment.

"Okay," I shrugged.

"There once lived a whale in the ocean. Now this whale was different than other sea creatures. He was smarter than the other whales and far more curious about the world around him. One day, he heard a legend about a fabled golden sea. A paradise filled with the most splendid sights imaginable. Well, as you can imagine, once he heard about such a magical place he couldn't resist finding out more about it. He began to dream about this golden land; he became obsessed. The whale knew he had to see this sea for himself. So he asked the fish, 'Where is the golden sea?' But the fish didn't know. He asked the squid, 'How can I get to the golden sea?' But the squid did not know either. No one had actually seen this sea for themselves."

Hiro chuckled as our waitress dropped off our drinks. He drained his glass immediately. He looked like he had been drinking long before we arrived. This man was unstable.

"The whale wasn't content to leave the mystery alone. So he continued to search for many years. One day, he happened to come upon a cove, a small inlet where dolphins liked to play. He searched every corner of the cove with his large whale eyes, but he found nothing that interested him. However, when he turned to leave, the whale found that the tide had fallen, and he was trapped."

Hiro motioned for another drink.

"As the water continued to recede, the whale found that he was beached. Eventually the sun started to bake his tender blubber. It was too hot, and he was ready to pass out when carrion birds came and began tearing into his flesh. The giant whale started to weep, but not because he was dying. Because the golden sea of sand he now lay on was the most beautiful sight he'd ever held. This was his golden sea. The whale had finally discovered the place that consumed his dreams, and it had only cost him his life."

I took a giant sip from my Beam and coke. I didn't know what to say.

"You were told that story as a child?" Shinji exclaimed.

Hiro ignored him.

"You've come to me for help," Hiro said looking at me. "Are you sure you're not looking for your golden sea?"

"I just want to understand," my voice cracked.

Hiro frowned; apparently he'd expected something more from me.

"Dexter approached me," he said, suddenly serious. "I don't know where he got the original programming."

"Original programming?" Shinji jumped in. "So Dexter had written some of it before he approached you?"

Hiro nodded. "Quite a bit, in fact. Dexter knew his way around neural networks, and he was good with genetic algorithms."

"So why did he come to you?" I asked.

"Instead of some other washed up scientist? Is that your question?" Hiro shrugged. "Dexter thought I was the best. Or he assumed I was the most opportunistic. Perhaps, I was the only one who would tell him that his dream wasn't impossible."

Hiro leaned back in his chair and began scanning the room for our waitress.

"So you decided to help him?" I prodded.

"As I said, he approached me. Originally he just wanted advice."

"What kind of advice?"

Hiro sighed. "Advice on evolved programming."

Shinji perked up. "I'd love to see your research."

"That's nice. You can't," Hiro said, staring Shinji down.

"I'm sorry?" Shinji said surprised.

"No apology necessary."

"No, I mean, why can't we look at your work?"

"That's the question you should have asked the first time," Hiro said playfully. "But it has nothing to do with what I want. There's nothing to see. We dismantled the Evi project. I burned it all."

"Why?" Shinji exclaimed.

"Evi was a disaster. It deserves to be forgotten."

"Excuse me," I jumped in. "Evi isn't gone. I think Dexter left some of the program at our office."

"And I told you to destroy it," Hiro said slamming one fist against the table.

The bartender looked over with a frown. She looked like she was ready to kick Hiro out the door.

"Mr. Valentine," Hiro added. "If Dexter was truly your friend, he wouldn't have wanted to share Evi with you. That program is…unnatural. It eats away at your insides. It…"

He trailed off.

Hiro flagged down our waitress for another drink, and to my surprise, she brought one to him immediately. He steadied the glass with both hands as he brought it to his lips. I could see in his eyes that he wasn't with us anymore. He was looking at something that only existed in his memory. He had painted over his erratic demeanor with a fresh coat of panic. The stench of fear boiled off of him like a gazelle caught under the claws of a wild cat.

I waited for him to say something more, to give me any details about this program that had terrified him so much. He offered nothing for free. We stared at each other, measuring one another's determination.

"Professor Hojo, please. I would like to believe that I knew my friend well, but if what you're saying is true, then it sounds like Dexter was conspiring behind my back. I just want to know what my friend was doing."

"Playing God," Hiro chuckled. "Your friend was playing God."

Shinji and I exchanged worried looks.

"Evi isn't just a program," Hiro added. "It's a life form."

"A life form?" I said dubiously.

"You are both programmers?" Hiro asked.

Shinji and I nodded.

"Then your understanding of life is probably too limited. You know the principles of Boolean logic, I'm sure. You know the "and," "or," and "not" equations taught to every second year computer engineering student. You probably understand the difference between a brute force algorithm and a minimax algorithm. Maybe you've even had one of those programming nightmares that are filled with endless scrolling lines of bytecode. Yes, you're probably very capable mathematicians. But the probably with mathematicians is that they rarely stop to think about—"

Hiro paused to sip his drink.

"They never think about how – for all their complexity – machines are really very limited? Nature's computers have never been as inefficient as man's."

"Nature's computers?" I asked.

"The human body," Hiro said. "You see God was a pioneer in engineering. A human cell can continue to function even after it has been damaged or compromised. Organic tissue is self-organizing. A person with a missing hand will continue to use brain tissue that controlled that hand in the past. And while nerve tissue doesn't re-grow, a lame person may learn to walk again if those neural synapses are rerouted. The body is a self organizing, self learning, and corruption-resistant system. No human engineered device sees results like that. Our designs are faulty."

"So you and Dexter were trying to create a computer out of living tissue?" I asked.

"No, no. Nothing so Mary Shelley. But those design philosophies were at the heart of Dexter's creative impetus? That desire to be like God. That desire to create a program a little more..." He sifted around for the right word. "Organically."

"Incredible." Shinji exclaimed with a realization. "Evi is an evolved program."

"What does that mean?" I asked.

Hiro looked away.

"Evolved programming was initially pioneered in the early days of artificial intelligence," Shinji offered. "It goes as far back as the 1960's. I know that some designers have tried to use the process for design purposes, but I had no idea that it was being used for advanced AI."

"It hasn't been used to developer advanced AI," Hiro said. "Not like this."

"I'm sorry, can we back up," I said. "What are we talking about here?"

"Dexter told me that he used a population-based metaheuristic optimization algorithm to gather his base code," Hiro explained.

"Okay," I said, more lost than before "Uh, what does that mean?"

Hiro sighed. "In the most basic of terms, evolved algorithms follow simple Darwinist principles: reproduction, mutation, and natural selection. A population of code is mutated over the addition of random values to each vector component–"

I stopped him again.

"I'm sorry professor. I need the third grade abstract."

Hiro stiffened. He must have thought I was an idiot.

"Here's all you really need to know. If you randomly change a piece of code long enough you eventually end up with something that starts to work."

"If you put enough chimpanzees in a room with typewriters…" Shinji offered.

"They'll eventually write the complete works of Shakespeare," I finished.

"Similar," Hiro added. "Genetic programming is a systematic method for getting computers to automatically solve a problem. Think of it as a design philosophy. The theory behind it all is simple Darwinism. I've helped evolve search programs by mating different sets of code."

"How do you mate code?" I asked.

"A base algorithm is mutated by combined it with random bits of code. This often results in gibberish. In fact, your first several generations never produce the results you're looking for, but by random chance a few will come closer to your intended design than others. It's survival of the fittest after that. The best results are kept to mate again, and their 'genes' are swapped. I've seen evolved search engines that had to be mated for 20 to 30 thousand generations before the system found a workable design. Of course, given the speed with which computer codes mates, this can be completed in a matter of days."

"The craziest part is that some of these evolved programs work better and faster than hand-coded algorithms," Shinji jumped in.

"No," said Hiro. "The craziest part, is that if try to read an evolved algorithms code, it doesn't make sense. It might appear to be a scrambled mess."

I sat stunned. This was exactly what we had experienced with Evi.

"So this is how Evi was created," I said.

"No, that is nothing like Evi. Evi is an anomaly."

"I'm sorry, I'm confused," I said. "I thought you were telling us how you designed Evi?"

"No, I told you how Dexter designed Evi."

"But, didn't you say you had helped him."

"I said, I tried. When Dexter came to me, the primarily Evi program was intact. He wanted my help replicating the creation."

"So, he didn't understand how it had happened the first time?" I guessed.

"No, he didn't. I tried to help him duplicate his mistake several times, but we failed in every attempt. None of our programs were as compelling or intelligent as Evi. That program remains unique. Whatever programming secrets Dexter used on Evi – whatever dark magic he evoked to create that monster – died with him."

I felt like I was finally getting a picture of what happened to Dexter before he died. Maybe Evi wasn't something Dexter created in secret. Maybe it had been an accident, and he was just keeping it hidden until he understood it. Maybe the program had cracked him before he cracked it.

"So that's it?" I pushed. "Evi is unexplainable?"

"Yes," Hiro continued. "But it's all for the best. Trying to replicate Evi was a mistake."

"Why do you keep saying that?"

"Mr. Valentine. You have to understand that Evi isn't a person. It doesn't think like a person. It doesn't communicate like a person. So when people try to interact with it like it is a person, it affects them in unnatural ways."

I frowned, that didn't make since, but I had experienced that firsthand.

"How could it do such a thing?" I asked.

"Fear," he said.

"Fear?"

"Evi is a beast that feeds on, even controls, your fear."

Hiro raised his hand to order another drink, but the waitress ignored him. They were finally cutting him off.

"What scares you, Mr. Valentine?"

What scared me? That was a long list: the thought of dying alone, quiet nights, the evil click of a loaded gun, my own internal beast. Right there, right then, what I feared the most was the thought of waking up on a day where the sun was out, my wife was alive, and life was beautiful, and then having to relive my experiences all over again.

"I don't know," I said.

"Don't be proud of that. A man has to understand his fears before he can understand himself." He leaned in close to whisper. "And if you don't understand your fears, Evi will use them to destroy you."

With that he stood.

"Wait, you're leaving?" I asked dumbly.

"I have to go."

"But I still don't understand."

He shook his head and swallowed a chuckle. It sounded like the cough of a dying man.

"You shouldn't understand."

With that, he staggered to his feet and began a long shamble to the door. The bartender yelled at him about his tab, but I waved at her, signaling that I would pay.

"How much do you think he had to drink?" I asked Shinji.

Shinji shrugged.

"Did you get what your needed?" he asked.

"I'm not sure," I mumbled.

We turned over cash for Hiro's hefty tab, then Shinji and I headed for the door. We heard the crash before we saw the accident. Breaks squealed and then there was an awkward thud. We were two seconds short of seeing everything.

Just outside, a convertible idled in the middle of the road. The car's hood was dented slightly. Its windshield a snowflake of fractures. Behind it a block worth of traffic was starting to build.

A chubby man with glasses walked up beside us.

"Did you see that? That little Asian dude went crazy," he said in shock. "He looked at the car speeding down the road and started running at it."

The driver paced beside his vehicle. Alarm poured from his mouth into a car phone. At his feet lay a familiar contorted form.

"It's like he wanted to get hit," said the excited man with glasses.

A large pool of blood was already forming underneath Hiro's limp body. In the distance I heard a siren's wail.

CHAPTER FIFTEEN: JACK & DEXTER

"A gun?"

"Yeah, why not." Dexter had said.

I looked down at the brown-handled revolver sitting atop confetti shreds of birthday paper.

"You always know just what I want," I had said sarcastically.

"I figured we could go to the firing range sometime," Dexter had said. "Drink some beers afterwards. Feel real manly."

He clapped me on the shoulder. Dexter had been to the range with his grandfather about a month beforehand, and for a period, many of his interests involved controlled explosions and targets.

"It'll be fun," he had said.

We never went.

My gun sits lonely in an empty sock drawer.

Dexter was a shifting entity. A personality of fizzling desires. He'd be hot about a particular fad, then suddenly cold about it a week later. It made him hard to gauge. He was a person of many unique parts.

He was a stocky, brown-haired savant with a special aptitude for anything he touched. He had wrestled in high school, and still had some of the build, but it was the build of a man who had stopped caring years ago. His hair was always a mess – a perpetual bird's nest – but he pulled it off like a rock star. His fingers were short and stubby like the rest of his body, and he complained that his hands had kept him from mastering a musical instrument even though he'd never really tried to learn one.

But Dexter was more than DNA.

He was raised in an unstable upper-class home. His family was old money – wealthy since America was a baby. His father loved his fortune more than his son. His mother loved her vodka more than her husband. She died when Dexter was a child, and he was raised by a rotating cast of Hispanic nannies.

But Dexter was more than poor breeding.

He went to one of the premier elementary schools in the nation. This third grade curriculum included classical piano and French. Later, he attended a boarding school in Connecticut that housed a world-class chef, a film studio, and two ice rinks. When he was seventeen, he spent a semester abroad in Europe. His father made him attend Notre Dame. Dexter tolerated it for six months, before transferring to Cal Tech.

But Dexter was more than an expensive education.

We met in college. Dexter was a computer science major, and we had several classes together. But it wasn't until our third semester that we got to know each other. I didn't realize that I'd been sitting next to my best friend for years.

When Street Fighter II came to arcades, we both became obsessed. It got so bad that we couldn't do our class work; we were playing the game too much. One time, during Linear Algebra we both completely broke down. I looked over at him, and I knew he was stringing together button combos in his head. Neither of us was in any condition to study vector spaces.

I passed him a note that simply read, "Street Fighter?"

He looked at me and smiled, then passed the note back.

He'd written, "I can take you with Ryu."

We both got up and walked out in the middle of class without saying a word. The rest of the students – including the teacher – stopped to watch us go.

We played Street Fighter the rest of the day.

Dexter obsessed over all form of entertainment: movies, books, word puzzles, board games. He took his entertainment in sets of two; he couldn't digest it fast enough. He would listen to music while he read. He would leave the TV on while he studied. He would watch movies and play computer games at the same time. He read comics and filled out crosswords in the middle of D&D sessions.

But Dexter was more than his addictions.

Dexter constantly challenged my views. If I said a game was bad, he would counter that the game was fine; it just didn't appeal to my appetite. When I said I didn't like a certain genre, Dexter had me playing through similar titles until he found one I liked.

Once time, I said that a particular video game developer was a sellout because it had made a terrible movie based on its property. Dexter told me that it was actually important for the industry's image to do a big film every now and then, even if the movie sucked.

Dexter said that I met him on an intellectual level. I just thought we argued a lot.

"I can't believe I only got a 'B' on this paper," he had complained once between classes.

"Well you did write it in one night," I'd said.

"Yeah, but it was a really intense night of work."

Dexter handed me his paper, and I flipped through his sermon.

Earth is a big place, full of exciting things, people, and places. Sadly, most of us will never see them. Confined to our prisons of asphalt, plastic, and paper, we are not as free to explore the treasures of this world as past societies. So much of our planet has already been charted. So man has turned to his digital devices, crafting experiences that fulfill his innate desire to explore. Video games are a necessary tool that appeases our need to conquer.

"I don't know about this, dude," I'd said. "I'm sure Marko Polo would have loved to take advantage of United Airline's frequent flier program."

"Sure we have better travel services today, but do we have the freedom that Marco Polo had?" Dexter had said. "We're too busy working at the speed of machines to go anywhere."

"You're saying we need games today because they give us a sense of freedom that we no longer have?"

"Sort of, I'm saying that video games – actually all games – are really about exploration. Games have always been about transporting their audience into different worlds – into different experiences and emotions."

"Yeah, but Dex, that's not exclusive to games. Books and movies provide symbolic adventure too."

He held up a finger to stop me.

"That's passive fantasy fulfillment. Games are a participatory experience. They're the only art form that allows the audience to actively explore the world and leave a personal impact on it."

I threw up my hands. "Well why don't you write another paper on that?"

He smiled.

"No, I'm done writing papers. I'm gonna make a game about this."

Dexter scored 2400 on his SATs. He spoke English, French, and Japanese. At the age of three, he was reading his own bedtime stories. While most kids were drawing spaceships, Dexter was drafting plans to build one. While most teens were worshiping Michael Jordan and Batman, Dexter was studying the works of Copernicus and Einstein. And Batman. He learned Trigonometry and practiced Fractals before he could drive. He even wrote a 30-page research paper entitled *The Magic of Vedic Mathematics and the Controversies Surrounding the Ancient Shulba Sutras* before he was legally able to drink.

But Dexter was more than his IQ.

As soon as Dexter got an idea into his head, you couldn't change his mind. Dexter wouldn't touch fish, and I don't just mean he wouldn't eat it; Dexter wouldn't go near the creatures. His romances were always short lived affairs. Normal conflicts that were healthy for most couples would tear his relationships apart. Dexter rarely fought for what he wanted, and when he did it usually drove someone away. Given his intellect and birthright, Dexter could have been a legend in the field of mathematics. He could have worked on the cutting edge of any scientific field, but all he wanted to do was make video games. It drove his father mad.

But Dexter was more than squandered opportunities.

"You know what I've been thinking about?" Dexter said one day while we were working late at the office.

"What's that?" I had asked not looking up.

"Throughout all of human history, everyone has played games: card games, board games, whatever."

I shrugged.

"Yeah, I suppose."

"Every age. Every race. Every sex, throughout the entire passage of human existence."

"So?" I said finally looking up.

"So, why did they suddenly become exclusive once they became electronic? Why do only geeks play video games?"

He made air quotes with his hands around the word electronic.

"I give up. Why?"

"I don't know either," he said cocking a wry smile. "I guess, you'd have to figure out why people play games in the first place?"

For some stupid reason, that question stuck with me. I couldn't stop thinking about it. I wanted the answer.

Why do we play games?

"Because they're fun," may be true, but it doesn't fully explore the heart of the issue. Was there a greater purpose to playing a game? What is it about adulthood that makes us view games as a child's exercise? What makes one game better than another? Why does one man love chess and hate baseball, while another finds chess a trial of his patience and feels no greater thrill than at a tailgate party before the big game?

I had thought that games' true function could be seen by looking at their earliest incarnations. But how far back would I have to look? Chess could be dated back to the seventh century, and checkers to 2000 B.C. The ancestral remains of Backgammon have been found in ancient Samaria, preserved for more than five thousand years. All history could tell me was that games were old. It couldn't tell me why we played them.

It took a trip to the zoo for me to realize that the history books didn't go back far enough.

Dexter and I were on a double date. Jill and her friend went off to find the bathroom when Dexter and I went to look at the lions. A lioness had given birth that spring, and the whole family was out enjoying the cool morning air. I watched one of the cubs – crouched under tall grass – creep slowly towards his brother. With a wiggle of his haunches, he pounced on his prey. The two infant lions started to growl and bite each other as they begun a playful wrestle.

A little girl next to me started giggling, and her mother explained how the lions were just having fun.

"This is how they play," she said.

A revelation sent me spinning. I would never find the origin of games by looking at human history, because games weren't a human invention. They predated us.

The girl's mother was right; the cubs were having fun. But their games weren't pointless. These lions were practicing the hunt. They were honing their survival skills – learning how to approach prey unseen. How to pounce. How to grapple and subdue without causing personal injury.

What's more, they were doing it all within a controlled, safe environment.

Their game was a psychological pretense to learn. Play offers the benefit of conflict experience without the physical, mental, and emotional consequence. It was better to make a mistake while playing against the young claws of a sibling rather than on the horns of a grown wildebeest fighting for its survival.

The benefit was likely the same for humans?

Thousands of years ago a hunter had to invent creative and personal ways to tutor his son in the craft of killing wild meat. It was important that he teach his children how to subdue and care for the Earth, but at such a young age how would they have kept their children's attention? Certainly, they didn't sit them at desks and lecture from a chalk slate. Games are the most primal, time-honored education technology. Schools were the innovative fad, the human created institutions that violated tradition.

Games allowed people the freedom to safely explore the anti-societal behaviors of violent, lewd, or dangerous situations. They fostered social interaction, provided mental and physical exercise, and sated our human hunger for acknowledgment and reward.

I would never feel bad again about cutting class to play Street Fighter.

While the cubs played, I explained my theory to Dexter.

"Too bad real work isn't a game," he nodded.

"You say that now, but once we teach a robot to program, we'll be out of a job."

I laughed at my own stupid joke.

Dexter didn't.

"You think that will ever actually happen?" he asked.

"That what will happen?"

"You think a computer will ever be able to create its own game?"

I shrugged.

"I guess it's possible. At this rate who knows. Maybe someday we will have machines making machines. Maybe we'll have auto-programmable programs. Maybe all our technology will be on this giant automated treadmill, propelling itself into progress without the need for humanity…God, that's scary."

I laughed again at the overwhelming giantess of it all.

Dexter didn't say a thing. He stared down a path toward the monkey habitat.

There was a long silence, and I leaned against the rail. One of the cubs had crawled between two rocks to hide, but his butt was sticking out and he was clearly visible. His brother rolled over him in excitement.

I was about to ask Dexter if he wanted to go find out what had happened to the girls, when I heard him whisper.

"Automated programs?"

"What?" I said turning to him.

He was staring at me, but not really at me. He was staring through me. I waved my hand in front of his face.

Slowly he came back.

"You okay?" I asked.

He smiled.

"Yeah, I guess I just got lost in my own science fiction."

But it wasn't science fiction. I didn't realize it at the time, but he was thinking about how he could actually do it. He was thinking about how he could actually make a program that programmed itself – about how he could teach a computer to play games. What I had thought of as an offhand comment, Dexter saw as an idea that demanded his creative force. To him automated programming was a real puzzle, something he would work to solve until the day he died.

Dexter was a complex guy, filled with mysterious thoughts and feelings he never shared. He was smart. He was funny. He was a man of many intricate parts.

But Dexter was more than the sum of his parts.

He was my friend.

CHAPTER SIXTEEN: GHOSTS

The cops arrived as the ambulance closed its doors and whisked Hiro towards Alameda County Medical Center. I hung around to answer their questions, and learned whatever I could about Hiro's condition. He hadn't died when he'd collided with the pavement, but he would end up in the ICU with a shattered spine. What a stupid way to not kill yourself, I thought.

My pager went off. It was Claire. I'd forgotten about her.

My world was in freefall. I'd just watched a man try to kill himself, then been grilled by the police for almost an hour. My career was in jeopardy. My best friend was dead, and his father had just stolen my company. The sun was setting, and my sweat-soaked clothes were starting to make me shiver. My breath tasted like whiskey, and my shirt smelled like cigarettes. I was tired. I was hungry. I wanted to be alone.

I was late for a date.

01000101010101011001001001

When I arrived at my apartment Claire was flicking through channels on the television. She didn't even look up as I walked in. She was so mad she wasn't even going to yell at me. After the standard pedestrian greeting and awkward silence that accompanied our every meeting, I gave her my excuses. I told her about David Hayward's takeover, my meeting with Hiro, and his accident. After my quick trip under a showerhead, she seemed to have forgiven me, though she kept asking me how I felt. I felt guilty for liking it better when she was just angry at me.

We'd missed our reservations at a steak place I had been planning to take her, so Claire drove us to one of our favorite Italian restaurants. The restaurant was called Luigi's – a rustic, little mom-and-pop eatery that had been crammed into a space barely large enough for a coffee shop. The Italian flag hung over the kitchen entrance, and on quiet nights, in the front room, you could hear the kitchen staff fighting. However, there were rarely quiet nights at Luigi's. The place was so popular that it could get as crowded as a Tokyo subway.

That night it was rush hour. The kitchen's metal door swung wildly like a flag in the wind. Piles of dirty dishes went through in one direction and seconds later steaming plates filled with delicious aromas came out. The restaurant's small wait staff buzzed through the restaurant, and delivery boys jogged back and forth along the store's main artery, dodging through the crowd of waitlist patrons that had spilled outside.

You didn't go to Luigi's for the atmosphere; you went for the heaping piles of perfect pasta and slow-cooked sauce.

We sat near a middle-aged couple who looked fairly well-to-do. Our tables were so close they almost touched, and I felt like I was sharing a meal with two people I'd never met. The woman wore a pearl necklace that matched her earrings and a haughty frown. The man – who sat elbow to elbow with me – hungrily, stuffed bread into his large gut. His girth was such that every now and then – as he brought a forkful of pasta to his lips – he would elbow my chair. When he did, I glanced over at him and he pretended not to notice.

Claire was better at ignoring our unwanted companions.

"So, how are you holding up?" she asked after we'd ordered our appetizer.

I said, "Huh?" as though I hadn't understood her. It was a pointless stall.

"You know. You've had a lot to deal with lately. How are you feeling?"

"Well, it looks like I'll have a lot more free time on my hands now," I said sarcastically. "So I guess I can relax a little."

I threw on a fake smile.

She ignored it and took a sip of wine.

The man next to me elbowed my chair, and I shook my head.

"I'm okay," I confessed.

"Yeah?"

"Yeah. I'll be okay. I mean, I am okay. I'll survive."

I didn't know what else to say.

"What are you going to do about work?" she asked.

"I don't know. I'll figure something out."

"It's not fair. You can't let Mr. Hayward—"

"Claire," I said a little too briskly. "I don't want to talk about it right now."

"Okay," she said retreating.

She took another sip of wine while she considered what to say next.

"Have you been sleeping alright?"

"I sleep fine."

Claire frowned. She knew I was lying, but she wouldn't press me.

"How are you doing?" I asked.

"I'm okay."

I settled back into my seat and we sipped wine in painful silence. Claire frowned, and I struggled for a way to fill the awkward hole between us. I felt like reaching over and holding her hand, but there was a physical barrier between us. I wanted to cross the table and kiss her, but our relationship wasn't that intimate anymore. It was a non-sexual relationship.

Not anymore.

"Jack, I'm lying," Claire said. "The truth is I'm not okay. I'm worried."

"Oh," I said trying not to panic.

"I'm worried about us."

I panicked.

She leaned forward, ignoring the couple next to us.

"It's just, you're never happy, Jack. You never seem to enjoy yourself when we're together."

I couldn't help but look over at the strangers next to us. I certainly wasn't enjoying myself in that moment. I drained the rest of my wine; it rested queasily next to the remains of the two beam and cokes I'd had at the strip club. The image of Hiro's car-dented body flashed in front of me, and I suddenly felt like I might puke up half my upper intestines.

"I feel like there is a growing distance between us," Claire continued. "I feel like you're always someplace far away."

Were we really going to do this here? Now?

"I'm right here," I said trying to be charming, but my chair shook as the man next to me accidentally nudged it, and irritation leaked through my voice.

"But I don't feel like you are here. I never know what you're thinking. Or what you're feeling. Sometimes when we're together I feel like I'm still alone."

I understood exactly what she meant. I felt that way no matter who I was with.

Claire looked as if she wanted me to say something, and I looked out the window hoping she wouldn't say anything more. A homeless man stared back at me from across the street. We locked eyes. I didn't want to face Claire; it was easier to face society's failures.

"Jack, please say something. What are you thinking?"

"Claire, I'm dealing with a lot of junk right now. My best friend just died and I lost my job. Can we talk about this later?"

I spoke softly, almost meekly, only willing to look at her reflection in the wine in front of us. It was a weak defense.

Our relationship was a mess for many reasons, but Dexter wasn't one of them.

"Do you find me attractive anymore?"

Claire's voice quavered, and her eyes were pooling. She remained poised, but she was only a single word away from breaking down.

"What?" I asked, finally looking straight at her.

"Are you attracted to me?"

My mouth dropped. I couldn't answer that. It was stupid. The woman with the pearl necklace was watching us now. Her conversation had long since stopped. Ours was more entertaining.

"It's just..." Claire continued hesitantly. "We rarely kiss. Sometimes you seem almost repulsed by my touch. And we never–"

"Don't." I shook my head.

"We never have sex anymore, Jack. What's wrong with us?"

An angry flash came over me, but I was too aware of the prying eyes next to us. I tried to be discrete, leaning forward and keeping my voice down.

"What kind of relationship do you think we're capable of? Not a normal one. What do you want from me?"

"I want you to act like you care about me."

She was beginning to raise her voice. The woman with the pearl necklace couldn't take her eyes off us. Was Claire trying to corner me in public? I felt my face flush.

"Look honey, I'm sorting through a few things Dexter behind, and right now–"

"Stop hiding behind the dead!" she yelled. "You say now's not a good time. Last week wasn't a good time either. Last month wasn't a good time. Will there ever be a good time, Jack? Will you ever care enough?"

My chair jiggled again as the man next to me reloaded his fork. My body went ridged as every muscle in my body clinched into a fist. I could hear the rumble of restrained energy in my own voice.

"Claire please, I am justifiably preoccupied. Dexter was working on this thing, this program–"

"He killed himself, Jack. He was depressed."

"No, there's more to it then that. There is an AI program. Something he called Evi–"

"AI program? Jack! This conversation isn't about Dexter."

Claire took a moment to breathe. The lady next to her was still enjoying her intimate view of our personal lives. I shot her a brief glance that said, "Mind your own damn business!" She ignored it.

Our appetizer arrived: bruschetta with roasted sweet red peppers. It would have been delicious, but we didn't touch it.

"I want you to answer a question," Claire said holding back tears. "And I need you to be completely honest."

The man next to me elbowed my chair. I felt sick.

"Do you love me?" she said.

Shit!

I took a deep breath then somehow managed to come up with an answer that was worse than "No."

"I…I don't know what I'm capable of feeling anymore."

Claire looked away. With a painted nail she brushed one tear from her eye.

Claire had always seemed distinguished – as powerful as royalty. Even then, on the verge of heartbreak, she'd never looked more beautiful than ever. Her head remained high as she kept perfect posture. Her skin glistened in the glow of dozens of small restaurant candles. Dark hair cascaded around her thin neck – a raven frame for her subtle, angular features. She could have had any man; why did she even bother with me?

Something terrible was happening. As I sat in front of a wasted appetizer watching Claire cry, the emotions I'd carefully chained down for so many years began to slip out of their shackles. I realized the answer to Claire's question. Yes. Of course, I loved her. I had for a long time.

Now it was too late.

While my passion was eating through my belly, an ugly snake began uncoiling under Claire's skin. I had been feeding it venom for years, and soon the killer inside her would strike back.

"I'm sorry Claire," I tried. "I'm a mess. Dexter committed suicide. Do you know how many memories that brings up?"

"Jack, do you realize how selfish you sound?"

She didn't bother catching her tears anymore.

"You're right," I said meekly. "But I keeping thinking that maybe I'm partially to blame. I feel like I should have seen this coming. Like I should have known what my friend was going through. I should have stopped it."

"Are you sure you're talking about Dexter?" she spit. "And not Jill?"

I reeled back. The serpent went for the throat.

"The truth is, she's the one that's been keeping us apart all these years. Even though she's been dead, she's still alive to you."

"That's not fair–"

"You can't forgive her for killing herself, and you can't forgive yourself because you think you drove her to it."

I couldn't breath. Her poison was making my hands shake. For a moment, my vision went dark. Then the adrenaline hit my heart. My muscles tightened and anger rinsed away my paralysis.

The man next to me elbowed by chair again, and my hand snapped over to grab his arm.

"If you do that again, I will snap your arm off," I barked.

He gave me a shocked, innocent look. It didn't matter. I was already on my feet. My chair fell backwards to the ground somewhere behind me. I shot one long finger at the woman with the pearl necklace.

"And mind your own fucking business!"

Her mouth gaped in horror.

The restaurant's atmosphere dimmed.

I focused on Claire. My hand was open, pointed at her like a knife. I had the whole restaurant's attention, and I didn't know what to do with it. I wrapped my hand into a fist, and laid it at my side. There was nothing to say that was good, so I clenched my jaw.

"I'll walk home," still managed to leak out of my throat as I threw money on the table. A corner of one of the bills landed on the Bruschetta. Its edge would remain stained red – just one of the many things that would be scarred of that night.

The people next to us stared at each other. Now they were overtly trying to act like they weren't paying attention.

"So you're just going to leave?" Claire asked.

I said nothing as I turned on my heels.

"Damn it, Jack!" she screamed as she followed me out the door. "Don't ignore me."

I was halfway across the street before she made it outside. I'd twisted my ankle in a pothole, but limped stubbornly down the street trying not to show the pain.

Claire called for me. I could feel her presence somewhere far behind. Motionless. Waiting for me to turn around. She was right: about pushing her away, about Jill, about everything. I kept walking. Each step increased more than just the physical distance between us. I turned at the end of the block, and was out of her sight.

My head began to ache. My jaw was still clenched.

01000101010101011001001001

The memory was only two years old, but it was ancient.

As I walked home from Luigi's, I relived it. My mind replayed the events in real time. It was August. It was misting. Another woman's sweat was on my skin. I approached my apartment from the emptiness of a dark street, and, in my memory, the wind picked up.

I shivered with the chill.

The environment played its part. My building's front lock fought with me. It didn't want to let me in. The door hissed angrily as I forced it open. Two of the front hall lights were out, exactly like they had been two year before. I could feel the hall breathing – its walls expanding in the darkness. Even the stairs cackled behind me as I climbed them.

I put my key in the door. Its tumblers offered no resistance; the door was already unlocked. The apartment screamed silence. I couldn't see her, but I could smell her. The walls echoed her ghostly sobs. She was home. She was waiting for me.

And she was very unhappy.

I wanted to turn and run, but that wasn't how it happened.

I walked up to the bedroom door. Two years ago I had stood here and listened to her cry. That was the night she caught me. That was the night she followed me over to Claire's and witnessed my infidelity.

That was the last night I'd had sex with Claire.

I couldn't face my dead wife again. Only an inch and a half of wood separated me from her, but I couldn't open it. That strength had left me.

Her memory opened the door for me. The sobbing stopped, and with one clean motion the door swung away.

Even as a memory she was radiant. Even dead, stained by years of tears, she was more glorious than a battlefield. Her presence crippled me. She was like a powerful drug, overpowering me with uncertain fear just as the needle slipped in and the world slipped out.

I hoped, for a moment, that I would pass out. But that wasn't how it happened.

My throat – dry as gravel – belched out, "I'm sorry."

It didn't matter. She was angry, and she was shaking violently with despair.

A taste like cancer settled in my mouth.

"I love you," I said.

It was too late.

"Please forgive me," I pleaded.

She couldn't.

She asked me why I'd done it?

I didn't have an answer for her.

I could hear death hiding in her shadow, preparing to pounce. Then there was a gun in her hand, and I was alert to the intent in her eyes. The first time I jumped back from fear that she might shoot me. This time I prayed she would.

I willed her to point the gun at me. But that wasn't how it happened.

My dead wife pressed the gun to her head and pushed a bullet through her brain.

In the stillness of memory, I helplessly watched it all unravel in slow motion. The trigger pulled. The hammer dropped. The flame and bullet exploding in opposite directions. The gory effect of physics.

In my imagination I try to rewind it all. I try to stop her. But that wasn't how it happened. I held her all night, as her dreams drained from her skull.

CHAPTER SEVENTEEN: ROUND TWO, PROPOSAL

At more than 25-feet-per second, D.B. Hayward Network's state-of-the-art elevator rocketed me into the heights of San Francisco's Financial District. Just a few blocks from the Transamerica Pyramid, Mr. Hayward's offices may not have been as tall as the famous landmark, but it didn't sit under any shadows.

Not content to have merely one successful business, nearly twenty years ago, David had begun expanding his empire into real-estate and property management. He now owned everything from restaurants to sporting goods stores to an office supply chain. He needed an office large enough to hold his ego.

Even in a concrete forest of commercial structures, the Hayward building was a bold symbol of American profit. Home to nearly 100 different retailers and corporate offices, the building featured one four-star restaurant, five cafés, a bookstore, an indoor RecRoom complete with a pool, a two story indoor atrium, and a rooftop garden. A web of 18 elevators shuttled workers and visitors to and from a 300-car underground garage.

Seated atop all forty-three floors of steel, glass, and corporate filching was David Hayward's personal office – his throne room.

With the gentle sway of a docked ship, the elevator came to a stop and its metal etched doors glided open. I'd been a busy man that day, franticly running between banks and law offices in preparations for this moment.

I had spent time with Meryl going over our original contracts. She hadn't worked for us when Dexter and I originally signed them, and after looking it all over, she was surprised we had. There was no legal way out of the hole we had dug for ourselves. Our situation was worse than I ever realized. But here I was, hat in hand, at David's office. One last ditch effort to save the company. It was time to finish what Dexter had backed down from. I took a deep breath then charged forward.

I was immediately road blocked by Emmerich. Mr. Hayward's personal assistant strode out from behind two potted bamboo trees.

"Jack," he said in mock surprise.

"Mr. ... Emmerich," I replied haughty but hesitant.

I realized I didn't know his last name. Emmerich probably was his last name, for all I knew.

"You're here to see David?" he asked pointlessly.

He knew why I was here.

"Yes, I need to–"

"Unfortunately, Jack, he's a little busy right now. Why don't we schedule an appointment?"

With a practiced frown he tried to motion me back towards the elevators. I stood firm.

"He's going to have to see me now."

Emmerich put his hand on my shoulder, trying to look sympathetic.

"This is about what happened to the dev studio, isn't it?"

"This is about what happened to my dev studio," I corrected.

He signed.

"I'll be frank, Jack. I think it would be best if you took some time off. You don't look good, you could use a break."

"I haven't been sleeping well," I grumbled.

"Well, go home. Get some rest. We're not disbanding the company, just restructuring it. You'll be back to work before you know it. Let us handle the heavy lifting for awhile. Just think of it as a vacation. Right now, the only thing you need to take care of, is you."

He tapped my chest with one of his long, knuckly fingers. I pushed it away.

"Don't patronize me."

His hands shot up in defense.

"Whoa Jack, I'm not the bad guy here. I'm just the messenger. And I'm telling you, David is dealing with some important personal business at the moment. Now is not the best time–"

"Yeah? Personal business? Is that what he's doing? Well this is the most important business he has right now, and I feel like it's very personal."

I pushed my way through Emmerich's blockade. He grabbed my arm. The tone of his voice dipped – reaching an almost threatening octave.

"Come on Jack, let's be civil."

"How about civil action?"

I slid a business card into the breast pocket of his sport coat.

"That's my lawyer. You might be getting a call. The police have some questions about a break in at Dexter's house."

"Jack," he tried to say sympathetically, but it was just pathetically.

"I know you'd like to pretend that everything is cool – that you can just roll over me, steal my company and I'll just take it, but that's not what's going to happen."

Emmerich's jaw snapped shut. I'd never seen him struggle for words before.

"Oh, and one of my engineers says he's being followed. Was that you? Or did David have someone else trailing him?"

"I don't know what you're talking about," he said not looking me in the eyes.

"Sure you don't. Leave him alone."

Emmerich looked around to make sure we were alone. For a brief moment, I thought he was going to hit me, but then he edged forward and whispered.

"This isn't worth fighting for, Jack. Let it go."

"You know, I still owe you a concussion." I pointed to the scar on my forehead. "Should I collect on that now?"

I'd never dreamed of saying something like that before. It was the kind of gruff, balls out, take no shit, dialogue that Philip Marlowe might have used.

It felt wonderful.

I stared Emmerich down. I could tell that he feared me – if only a little. For a second, I thought about hitting him anyway, but I had more important business to deal with. I slowly reached for the electronic keycard attached to Emmerich belt and used it to open the glass door in front of us. He didn't even try to stop me. Before I turned the corner at the end of the hall, I glance back to see Emmerich's sad, worried figure staring at the floor. It was almost as good as hitting him.

My heels clacked over black ceramic tiling, and I passed rows of potted Bonsais before entering Mr. Hayward's reception area. His secretary – seated at a spacious cedar desk – stood as I breezed past.

"Good afternoon sir. How can I–"

I ignored her and cracked open the heavy wooden doors that read: David Hayward – Chief Executive Officer.

"Excuse me sir, you can't go in–"

But I already had.

The room was surprisingly Spartan. Inset bookshelves decorated with business and humanitarian awards lined both sides of the door. Original works of art spotted three of the walls, and an Indian rug gave the room a splash of color, but the room was so large that much of the office was empty space. Its scope was intimidating – like swimming next to a blue whale.

"Mr. Hayward, we need to talk!"

He was perched over his desk, hands spread out like tent poles, propping him over the cherry-stained mahogany. He looked up slowly through wire frame spectacles, but didn't say a word. His face was expressionless.

I charged forward.

"You exploited our contract. We weren't given fair warning – we didn't have time to make a counter offer."

"Now's not a good time, Jack," Mr. Hayward said dryly, looking back at the notes on his desk.

"You stole our computers."

Mr. Hayward hung his head and sighed.

"I'll have to call you back Mr. Bison."

"No problem, sir," came a voice from the speakerphone at David's desk.

David pushed a few buttons and the line clicked dead. His leggy secretary jumped forward.

"I'm sorry sir, he just barged in."

He waved her off.

"Don't worry, Cammy. It appears that Mr. Valentine and I have some important business to discuss."

David and I stared each other down as Cammy's high heels clicked out of the office. Once the double doors had clapped shut, David removed his reading glass, straightened his tie, and with a perfect Picard maneuver eased into his dark leather chair.

"Well have a seat, Jack."

He motioned to a smaller version of his chair on the other side of his desk.

I threw a business card on top of his work pile. It was a practiced move. I wanted to appear bold, but the card seemed small and powerless resting atop the sea of Mr. Hayward's papers.

"You came all the way up here to give me your card?"

"It's not mine. It's my lawyers. I came all the way up here to tell you that I'm prepared to take legal action against you."

"Then shouldn't your lawyer be here to give me his card?"

"No," I muddled. "Not yet. I just wanted you to know that I'm prepared."

"Jack," he said amused. "I spend more money on lawyers every year than your entire company was worth. You don't want to go toe-to-toe with me in a courtroom?"

I frowned. This was not how I'd hoped this would go.

"Mr. Hayward, we don't need to measure our cocks. I came here alone, hoping to appeal to your sensibilities."

"Okay, Jack. So what can I do for you?"

"You can sign this."

I threw a thick manila folder on his desk.

"I want to buy back all the software ESP owns. You get to keep the offices, the equipment, even the employees, if you want them. I just want the tech we developed."

David leafed through the papers, glancing at each sheet for only a fraction of a moment.

I looked out across the gorgeous view of Chinatown and the Bay Bridge, visible through the wall-length window behind David's desk. The sun poured through the window, spilling over David's shoulders in extra volumes of yellow. The glass seemed to make the light brighter than usual, or perhaps the sunshine was somehow less diluted. We seemed so much closer to the source.

David closed the folder.

"Jack, this stuff…" he said in a soft, friendly tone while waving the folder through the air like a flag. "…this can wait. These kinds of business deals take months of reevaluations and board meetings. But, I assure you that you and your people won't be losing your jobs. Just enjoy your time off."

"So you're just blowing me off?"

"Trust me; your programs are safe under my ownership. Electric Sheep has a rare opportunity to go through an exciting growth spurt. Who cares who owns what? I can tell the future holds some exciting things for the company. I'd like you to remain onboard for them."

He offered a devil's smile.

"Then why did you take away our computers?"

"That's just part of the evaluation process. I just needed you guys to stop working while we go through the books."

Bullshit.

"When can we have them back?"

"When the evaluation is over."

"This is an invasion of privacy."

Mr. Hayward leaned back in his chair and stared me down.

"Okay, Jack."

He threw up his hands in defeat then flicked open a digital planner.

"Your right, I should have included you in all the planning. That was my mistake. I have an open slot next Thursday, why don't we get together and I'll bring you up to speed—"

"Mr. Hayward, I didn't come down here to reschedule another meeting. I came to set a few wrong things right." Then at the last moment I added, "Your wrongs."

I pointed to the folder that now rested on his desk.

"You know why I'm here," I continued. "Let's not play games. I'm not here to get more involved. I'm here because I want out. The sums I've drafted up are more than fair."

"Okay, Jack. I'll have my accountants look over your offer."

He picked up the folder and set it delicately aside.

That wasn't good enough.

"You're not going to sign it are you?"

"Well, you haven't given me much time to consider."

"No," I said. "You're not going to sign, because you don't really want Electric Sheep. You never cared about our company, or my people, or what we did. Not even when Dexter was around."

Mr. Hayward crossed his arms and stared at me.

"The only reason you acquired our company was to get your hands on Evi. Am I right? You know about the AI don't you? You've know about Dexter's secret project longer than I have. That's why you wanted our computers. That's why you sent Emmerich to Dexter's house to fetch the Alpha build the night after he died."

I was making a wild educated guess hoping that David would confirm my suspicions, but Mr. Hayward didn't respond.

"Okay," I said. "You don't have to say anything. I've already pieced together most of the puzzle. I talked with a professor who was helping Dexter – did you know him?"

"…"

I folded my arms. It didn't matter that David wasn't answering my questions; I could answer some of them for him.

"Here's my theory: Dexter was a genius. A visionary. Even an artist when it came to the field of artificial intelligence, but when it came to practical business, he was clueless. He didn't know what to do with this program he'd accidentally discovered."

"…"

"He needed a financial backer to fund more research. So he came to you?"

"…"

"He came to you for help, and you stole his work."

David finally spoke.

"His needs were more than financial."

"Oh?"

"As you said, my son was a dreamer."

"I said, artist."

David gave me an annoyed nod.

"Dexter was never good at thinking about his future; he was always lost in his mind. So after he stumbled into Evi, he didn't know what to do with it. He came to me for money, yes, but he also needed connections – marketing knowledge – he needed to know what he could do with this program."

"You guys fought over it," I said with a revelation. "You both argued about what to do with Evi."

"I wouldn't call it that."

"But that's what it was," I continued. "If I knew Dexter, he would have seen Evi as an inspiration to programmers everywhere. Research on thinking machines has always been a neglected field, and Dexter would have hoped to change that. He would have wanted to safeguard his project from unscrupulous practices – to make sure that it was only used for good."

"'Used for good?' Jack, do you realize how naïve you sound? What good is science if no one benefits from it?"

"Yes," I said with an exclamation point. "That's exactly how you see things. After all, you don't waste money blowing up a mountain when you know it's filled with gold. You sell it to the highest bidder. The thing is, Dexter knew there was something wrong with his program. He wanted to research the problem. You wanted to sell it. You didn't understand that he was sitting on a bomb."

David's eyes became deadly slits. I was uncomfortably close to the truth. His silence drove me to a scary realization.

"Good God! That's it, isn't it? You think Evi can be used as a weapon?"

"That's a bit of an oversimplification."

I ignored him.

"That's why you and Dexter got into it. Dexter didn't want you raping his science for profit."

"I think I've heard enough."

But I wasn't done.

"So Dexter hid the program. He put it inside one of ESP's game builds, thinking I'd find it after he died."

I leaned forward and placed my hands on his desk to drive home my point.

"This morning I found a copyright for Evi that Dexter had filed under Electric Sheep's name. Your son died thinking you couldn't touch his software. He never imagined that his own father would break into his house and steal his research. He never suspected that you would exploit a forgotten contract to buy our company just to gain the copyrights."

"Okay, that's enough, Jack."

"You ripped the greatest scientific achievement of the century out of your dead son's hands."

"I said, that's enough!" David huffed with a red face. "I think it's time for you to leave. Go home and think long and hard about how much you care about your company. About how much you enjoy your job. And about how much you'd ever like to work in this field again."

"You're going to try and blacklist me?" I said. "I don't think so. Here's the deal: I'll go home, after you've signed those papers. I'll just disappear. You'll never have to see me again. You'll never have to meet my lawyers. And most importantly, I'll never tell anyone about all your evil secrets: how you lied, cheated, and stole from your son. How you treated him like a stranger half his life. And how, when he was a child, you would get drunk and beat on him."

"What!"

"Dexter and I were friends for a long time, Mr. Hayward. He told me a lot of secrets."

"Get the hell out of here!"

I swallowed hard. There was something cold and surgical about the way he delivered the line. A part of me wanted to run from his office immediately. The stupid part of me decided to stay. This was my last power play. This was my attempt at meeting Mr. Hayward on a field he understood.

"Mr. Hayward, this isn't something I'm proud of, but if threatening your reputation is the only way to negotiate with you – if it's the only way you do business – then it's something I'm prepared to do."

He was silent for a moment. His head hung low, as the steam began to boil out his face.

"You think this scares me?" he said. "Do you think that this is the first time I've had to deal with threats?"

His face continued to redden, but his voice remained even.

"Jack, do you know how many times I've backed down?" He made a zero with his thumb and forefinger. "We are not negotiating. I'm where I am today, because I never back down."

I was suddenly consumed by an oppressive heat. I was sweating. Why was I sweating? I hoped David didn't notice the beads on my brow. I wanted to wipe them away, but I didn't want to draw attention to the fact that I was sweating. A large tear rolled off the top of my hairline.

This isn't how I'd hoped this confrontation would play out, but what had I really expected? Did I think this man would fold immediately under my bullying? I tried to think of something witty that would help me regain some ground, but there was nothing I could do at this point. So instead of speaking I shrugged. It probably looked pathetic.

I was a mouse to this man.

"Everything I have done since my son died has been for him," David continued. "The programming he did on Evi is amazing. It shouldn't work. You know that, don't you? The design doesn't make sense. According to everything my researchers have told me about the program, it shouldn't do anything. It's a miracle. The only mistake my son made was leaving it in the hands of an independent toymaker who won't have the vision to do anything with it other than make children's games."

David paused to lean forward and punched a few buttons on his phone.

"I've been told that this program is a revolution. That it will make a lasting impact on the world in ways we still haven't dreamed. Do you understand that, Jack? Have you thought about how this program might alter the fields of engineering or medicine? Do you understand the benefits this program will bring to our nation – to the world? There is a lot riding on the line here. My son's legacy won't be worth a damn without the resources I can provide."

I shyed back and nodded. Mr. Hayward was making a lot of sense.

"That is why I'm not going to sign your papers. That's why I'll never sign these papers." He stabbed the folder on his desk with his forefinger. "You would do nothing with my son's work."

I heard the door to David's office open, and someone with feet the size of a Clydesdale's, approached.

"Now, I've been very patient as you came in here, interrupted my business, and threatened me with ultimatums. But now I want you out of my building."

A gorilla with a man's face and a well-tailored suit grabbed my arm.

"Please come with me, sir," he said.

As the monkey began to drag me out of the office, I realized something. The way David had been talking about Evi – the things he'd said about the program – they seemed to imply that he wasn't very familiar with it.

"Mr. Hayward, have you actually seen the program?" I asked.

He took a sip of water from a crystal glass at the edge of his desk.

"Goodbye, Jack. Don't come back."

"You have other people analyzing it, don't you? You haven't interacted with it at all!"

A powerful body yanked on my arm.

"Mr. Hayward please, there's something wrong with Evi. It's dangerous. Look at it yourself. You'll see it's not normal."

But it was too late. I'd been dragged from his office like a crazy person.

CHAPTER EIGHTEEN: RESPONSIBLE ART

I felt like a VIP. I felt like an important person. I felt like a very important person. And in case I forgot, I had a badge on my shirt that told me how very important I was. It read: VIP. Pleased that my shirt could validate me in such a way, I strutted past rows of framed paintings.

After leaving David's office, I found myself in an art show. Claire's art show. Her art association had rented out an abandoned department store for the week, and the first floor of the entire building was stuffed with more canvas than a tent factory. After our fight, I wasn't sure if Claire still wanted me there, but she hadn't taken me off the VIP list, so I stood in what used to be the men's shoe department, munching expensive hors d'oeuvres, and looking at pretentious representations of modern art. I felt like a VIP. I felt like a real person. Like a very real, very important, and very drunk person.

Like a puppeteer trying to animate a bag of sand, I grabbed two salmon rolls from a passing tray and stuffed them into my mouth. Claire had been surrounded by her entourage since I arrived. She didn't even bother to look at me when I walked through the door. I didn't have the courage to approach her, yet.

Seven beers into art appreciation, an athletic Bohemian woman walked up to me. I don't remember how the conversation started, or how long we talked, but I remember the sparkle of her necklace – the icy jewel floating just above the low V of her blouse.

"What do you think of this one?" said the well-formed chest in front of me.

I had forgotten her name already.

The painting in front of us showed a couple of men in a construction site at dusk. One of them was pointing a gun at the other. It could have been any random drug deal gone wrong, except both men were unwittingly about to be swallowed by giant teeth being formed out of the unfinished building. The piece was entitled, *The Human Condition*.

"I get the feeling that the artist was hungry when he drew this," I said.

I could have framed her smile and put it on the wall next to the rest of the art.

"You're cute Mr. Valentine."

I blushed. If I hadn't been sloshed, it might have shown.

"I wasn't trying to be," I said.

She smiled again then placed her hand on my shoulder, leaving it there for a moment longer than she should have. I knew she was flirting with me – playing some game of charms. She seemed like the kind of woman who played with the heart of every man she met. As though she enjoyed seeing how quickly they fell under her spell. How long would she attend to me after I succumbed to her charms?

"I'd like to show you one of mine, Jack. Do you mind if I call you Jack?"

It was an absurd question, mostly because of the fact that it was my name. But I happened to enjoy the way she said it. She stressed the mid part of my name, letting the "k" float away slowly. It was musical. Intoxicating.

I nodded. She could call me whatever she wanted. I just wished I knew what to call her.

"Come here," she said.

She pulled me down the wall, giving my arm a light squeeze.

"Oh my, do you play sports?"

I didn't want to answer, and she didn't seem to need me to, because she kept the conversation going all by herself.

"You men, always chasing your balls."

"Well, they're easier to catch than women," I said.

She laughed: a few hearty palpitations trickling into a light giggle. She leaned forward, pressing her hand lightly against her stomach. The top of her blouse pitched forward, and I could see the lacy tips of her brassiere. Something she'd likely purchased to be seen.

I was feeding off her. I wanted to play her game. Something inside me stirred – the beast inside me growled.

We stopped at a painting entitled *The Violent Game in the Video Violence*. It was a bit abstract. From what I could tell, there was a monitor, or a television, or some kind of clear empty box with a jar lid screwed on top. Along the border of the painting was a violent hue of red and orange. I could make out vague images of people fighting, or people killing animals that all looked like small explosions. In the bottom right hand corner bloomed the black mushroom of an atomic cloud.

I hated abstraction.

"What do you think?"

"It's…good," I said, only slightly slurring my words. I was losing my buzz.

"I believe artists should retain a certain amount of responsibility in their work."

"Of course," I said.

Like a magnificent ponce, I nodded along. I was looking at her well-tanned cleavage again, still trying to remember her name.

"Newer media like TV and video games have altered the way we look at art. As artists, we need to be aware of how that offends the status quo. I'm presenting this piece as a wake up call. I want to change people's perception of art."

Whatever the hell that meant.

"Here's my theory," she continued. "Growing up I probably watched 100,000 hours of television."

I thought about my own childhood. I'd probably spent 100,000 hours playing video games.

"That must have affected me on some level," she said. "In the world of sitcoms, everything always works out just fine. As a kid, I was taught that every problem has a solution, and that all drama has some comical nature. Sitcoms instilled me with fluffy morals about family, and friendship, and laughter."

That wasn't my childhood. In the world of classic video games, the player is taught that they have to fight for their life from the very moment they are born into the world. While every problem has its solution, choices have repercussions – every action has consequences. Games taught me that I had to fight back. Self-preservation came first. But no matter how hard I fought, in the end, I always died.

"Sitcom babies have been raised to be passive. After each episode, things always return to normal. No problem ever has lasting consequences. We've been trained to blow off our problems, because we don't truly believe in penalties. We've created a generation of people who don't know how to deal with conflict."

You couldn't beat Pac-Man. You never finished Donkey Kong. Children of my generation played those old games until they ran out of quarters – until they'd used up all their lives. Those arcade kids grew up, and now our culture has a greater obsession with death and defeatism than ever before. It's almost like we created a generation of nihilists.

"That's why artists need to take more responsibility for their work," she finished.

What was this woman's name?

Suddenly, I caught a glimpse of Claire. She was only about twenty feet away, in a group of four people. The group erupted in laughter. Claire's smile could have lit up the sky.

I should have been standing there with her. I should have been laughing at her jokes. I should have been basking in her glow.

I looked up into my nameless woman's eyes. Until that moment, I hadn't noticed their enchanting blue hue. I groped through alcohol's impairing haze and pulled a line – nearly word for word – from one of Dexter's old college papers.

"You talk as if art is a dangerous instrument, but it's only dangerous because it makes us challenge our beliefs."

"That's what I mean by taking responsibility–"

"But you've got it backwards. Art isn't a threat to society. Society is a threat to good art."

She looked slightly flustered. I was changing the rules to her game. I wasn't supposed to challenge anything she said.

"But don't you think artists need to be held responsible for how they influence our society?"

"Why?"

She was stunned speechless that anyone would even question that.

"If there is one thing I've learned from history," I said. "It's that things never stay the same. One generation's reproach inevitably leads to acceptance. Children are always more accepting than their parents, and children will undoubtedly expand an art form into something their parents hate. Perceptions don't need to be willed to change; the cycle is too big to control."

"But you can't argue the fact that our entertainment is more violent now than it's ever been."

I laughed; it was sobering.

"Of course I can. Haven't you ever seen Giotto's The Last Judgment? Or listened to accounts of Roman gladiatorial events? Or read the Bible? We're violent beings. It's in our genetics. Violence has always been our entertainment."

"But...doesn't that scare you," she said with a gasp. "If art affects people in such powerful ways, shouldn't we, as artists, be responsible for censoring our work?"

The group surrounding Claire wandered off. She was alone now. This was my opportunity. It was time to end this flirtatious game.

"I don't think so. Sometimes people need to be offended. The fact that art is dangerous means it genuine. A good artist is able to speak truth into a stale, aging society; a society that has forgotten why it obeys certain laws or conforms to certain social structures."

I began to raise my voice. Suddenly, I was angry. Angry at the spoiled artist in front of me. Angry at the world for being so stubborn. Angry at myself for more reasons than I understood.

"We shouldn't be censoring ourselves," I said standing a little taller. "Not while we're trying to inspire each other to grow – not while we're trying to show each other love and beauty. This world is filled with so many sharp edges I spend most of my time bandaging wounds. I don't want to drink my beauty from a sippy cup; I need to bath in it."

I stopped to breathe. The woman in front of me looked at me like she was seeing me for the first time.

"Now, if you'll excuse me, there is someone else I need to speak with."

There was a sparkle of nervous energy in her eyes as I turned to leave. She looked very alone, as though this was the first time in a long while that she wasn't the one walking away. She didn't know how to react.

But, walking away from people was something I was good at.

I didn't give her another look as I made my way across the storefront. My eyes were focused on Claire. She never looked over, but I'm sure she could hear me approach, given the pounding coming from inside my chest.

I tapped her on the shoulder.

"We should talk," I said.

Her faced drained, and for a brief second I saw undeniable fear.

"I have some things–" she started, pointing at the walls and trying to move away.

I grabbed her arm.

"Claire, please. I'm sorry."

She pulled close to me. Fear, excitement, and anger all welled up in her eyes.

She looked fragile – but she could subdue me with a glance.

CHAPTER NINTEEN: BAD MATH

"...Which got me thinking about several things these last few days."

"Like what?" she said with her arms crossed and her jaw set.

We stood in one of the back rooms of the empty department store. Bare clothing racks stretched – like dominos waiting to fall – toward a darkened loading dock. Just enough light filtered through the seams of its garage door for me to see Claire's soft hued features.

"I've been thinking about math," I said.

"Jack, I didn't agree to come back her so you could play games with me."

She motioned to leave.

"Wait please." I held up a hand to stop her. "I've been thinking about how, my whole life, I've been using this funny kind of math to make myself happy. Without really thinking about it, I've been acting like there was some kind of magic formula for happiness. If I added this or that to my life then I'd be happy. But all my best efforts to attain happiness only sabotage that goal."

Claire crossed her arms. I couldn't quite read her expression in the dim light, but I could see I was losing her. She didn't understand what I was going for.

"It's not like what I want is all that bad," I continued. "But I keep trying to stack up all these experiences, possessions, and relationships, and they always seem to add up to less than I thought they would. It's like happiness is a funny kind of math that I can't figure out."

"Jack, when are you going to let this all go?" She drew in a deep breath. "When are you going to forgive yourself for what happened with Jill?"

Her words plowed into me. I tried to swallow a hard lump in the back of my throat. My response was wet with anguish.

"We killed her, Claire. I killed her."

"Jill committed suicide, Jack."

"No." I shook my head. "She held the gun to her head, but we put it in her hands."

"You think our affair gave Jill the right to kill herself?"

"Not the right. No. But the reason," I said meekly.

"You think she's not responsible for her own actions because you were cheating on her?"

"That's not what I—"

"Jill was never a happy person, Jack. She'd been clinically depressed since the age of sixteen. Remember all the medication she took?"

"She stopped taking it," I said.

"Yeah, she stopped, and that's when things got worse. She was a basket case. Discovering your infidelity was merely the thing that pushed her over the edge."

"I don't see how you can justify our actions so easily," I said. "You didn't know her like I did. You never really understood her."

Bad math.

"You don't think I understood her!"

"You know what I mean, Claire."

"Damn it, Jack, she was my sister."

Claire punctuated her point by slamming an open hand against one of the empty racks.

"You don't think I cared about her?" she asked.

"No. I just mean—"

"You don't think that knowing I hurt her – knowing how we hurt her – caused me pain? You don't think I feel guilty for what I did?"

"Look, that's not what I meant."

"Well, what did you mean, Jack? You're not the only one who loved her. I cried myself to sleep every night for months, wishing I could take it all back. It took me a long time to get over hating myself, and it kills me to see that you can't do the same. You aren't honoring her memory by burying yourself under its shadow."

I was silent – afraid to speak. Afraid of what Claire might say next.

"Jack, you have this fairytale memory of what your life was like when Jill was around. You want to believe that you lived in this perfect little world, and now that she's gone, you'll never be able to be happy again. It was a dream, Jack. That old life wasn't real. It wasn't how you remembered it."

I threw up my hands.

"I know what's real. I know I had a needy, emotionally-deficient wife who was as bad at dealing with pain as I was at dealing with problems. I know that, in reality, our marriage wasn't perfect. But it was good. And I screwed it up."

Claire hung her head and stepped back. She took a loose strand of hair and looped it back over her ear.

"It's been two years, Jack. Eventually you have to move on. But you haven't. You're so full of sorrow it's made you sick. You're not living. You're just surviving."

"I didn't ask you back here so you could tell me what I'm doing wrong with my life."

"Yeah, well then why did you ask me back here?"

"For an apology."

"You have some nerve, Jack! You want me to apologize to you?"

"No – that's not – why are you always misreading everything I say?"

Our tones were quickly escalating.

"Why are you so pigheaded?" she yelled.

"I wanted to apologize to you!" I exploded.

The large open area echoed back with a shudder. I took a deep breath; the air felt thinner than normal.

Claire paused. I still couldn't read her face. What was she thinking?

"Okay…was that the apology?"

"…yes."

I searched for more words. I had a plan. I had had a plan. But the details were getting confused in its execution. I had planned on asking Claire for forgiveness. I had planned on telling her I was sorry for ever hurting her. I had planned on telling her I was sorry that I had used her as a crutch when my marriage soured. Then I had planned on telling her that I knew our relationship was a hallow romance – a courtship of obligation. We were two people fused together by tragedy. I had planned on telling her that I couldn't do it anymore, that she deserved more than I could give. I had planned on breaking her heart.

What I hadn't planned on, was that in the middle of all that, I'd start kissing her.

Bad math.

It happened spontaneously – action without thought. Our lips pressed tight. Our bodies colliding. Our hands groping about in the dark. God, she smelled good. I could feel her gyrate against me, feel her movements under the sheet of her dress. My intellect collided with my emotions, and lost. The beast inside me struggled against weak constraints – fought for control. I let him have it.

The ancient Greeks called this the madness of the gods. Eros: a passion that could drive men insane. In that moment, I was possessed by that ancient god of lust. I pushed Claire against one of the empty clothing racks. There was a small metallic click as a screw fell to the floor. I began kissing her; starting at her neck, then moving down.

"Oh, Jack."

She moaned my name softly, and it sent my stomach into zero gravity. I felt amazing, powerful. I needed her. I needed this. I started to slip off her dress and whispered her name.

"Jill, I love you."

Except it wasn't her name.

Bad math.

Her body went ridged. She grabbed my head and pulled our eyes level. I couldn't tell what emotion I saw in her eyes. Sorrow? Anger? Pity? I don't think Claire knew what she was feeling.

"Are you making love to me, or your dead wife?" she asked.

"I want you," I said breathing heavy.

"Jack, I honestly don't think I care at this point, but if we are going to do this, I need to know who you're thinking about."

Something nudged my stomach in an uncomfortable direction. The truth was that Claire and I had never made love. Sex wasn't love. Love was older and bigger than anything Claire and I had shared. It was such a massive concept it blew my mind. Kings and poets had been crushed under its power. Love was too civilized – too honorable – to be associated with our actions.

Claire and I had only ever fucked.

I didn't need to say it. Claire could read these thoughts off my face. She slapped me. And by the time I looked back up, a twinkle of tears had collected in her eyes.

"Claire–" I started gently.

She slapped me again. This time I didn't look back up right away.

"Tell me you love me," she said with a cracked voice.

"I do."

"No," she yelled. "That doesn't count. Say the words. Say, 'I love you'"

"…"

"Jack. Tell me you're not just with me because you feel bad about what happened to Jill. Tell me our relationship hasn't been built on guilt."

"I love you."

It was the right answer to the wrong question, and it was too late.

She shook her head. "I don't believe you."

"I don't know what to say anymore," I shrugged.

"You mean you don't know what to say without lying."

Her words popped out from under a mess of mucus and saliva.

I nodded.

That was it. We both knew what had just happened. There was no point in talking anymore. Claire's shoes had been thrown off during our brief moment of passion, so she moved to put them back on, smoothed out her dress, and then walked back into the art show.

I let her go.

Bad math.

I hung my head, and swallowed back desire. My body was tight and irritated. Even though she was gone, I could still sense her. She had left her smell – her taste – all over me. I still had the itch to feel the press of her skin under mine.

In a release of tension, I kicked over one of the empty clothing racks. It crashed into the one behind it causing a chain reaction of falling metal. The ruckus was deafening. Finally, the last rack landed lopsided against the loading dock door. Everyone at the art show must have heard the disaster.

I had to leave before I exploded.

But I didn't have time. Claire's brother Barry burst into the back room.

"What did you do?"

"It was an accident; I didn't think they'd all fall over."

Barry grabbed the lapels of my jacket.

"What did you do to my sister, asshole? She's crying. She won't talk to me."

Barry was a short Irish-looking man. He was quick to anger, and slow to forgive, and he looked like he'd been working out since I'd last seen him. We'd never gotten along very well, even before Jill's death.

"Nothing happened, we were just talking."

He leaned into my face, barring his teeth.

"Did you hit her?"

"What? No."

He punched me the gut, and for a second, I thought I was going to vomit up a serving tray of salmon rolls.

"Don't lie to me," he yelled.

I groaned my way into an upright position.

"Barry, I know you don't like me—"

"Don't like you?" he forced a laughed. "You're the reason one of my sisters is dead and the other is sad all the time. I hate you."

"Not as much as I hate myself," I smiled.

Bad math.

He backhanded me.

This time my belly flamed, and I punched him back. I couldn't help it; the motion erupted out of me in a reflex. It was almost the same thing that had happened when I kissed Claire. I was losing control of myself.

Barry bent at the knees and staggered back. He recovered, but he was drooling blood. He wiped it away with his left hand then laid into me with everything he had. I was down on the floor before I knew it. There wasn't much fight in me: just enough to get my ass kicked.

Barry started kicking me in the gut. He showed an incredible amount of restraint by not killing me. One stray boot landed on my cheek, and for a minute, I teetered on the edge of the black, but I came back in time to feel Barry kneel down on my chest and punch me across the jaw a few times. I'd had a lot to drink, but it wasn't enough; I would remember everything in the morning.

Barry stood and leaned over me.

"If you hurt her ever again, I will kill you."

Then the blurry towering visage thundered out.

I heard weeping, and it took me a moment to realize it was my own. I'd fallen pretty far. I'd lost my best friend, my job, and my girlfriend in one week. Now I was lying half-drunk and bleeding on a cold cement floor, wishing I'd just been killed. I curled up on the floor with my knees to my chest, and let the howling emotions inside finish the job Barry had started. My world was falling on top of me.

I'd been wrong about exploding. I was imploding.

CHAPTER TWENTY: SUBSONIC WAVES

The next morning I awoke on the floor next to my bed; I hadn't mustered the strength to travel the two extra feet and land on the mattress. In truth, I don't know how I got as far as I did. I don't remember coming home.

According to my watch – which had pinched its way up my arm, cutting off the flow of blood to my hand – it was one thirty-five. I pulled my chin off the carpet and felt the divots it left on my cheek before staggering to the window. Squinting under the sun's rays, I quickly drew the curtains closed. I was still wearing my dress cloths from the art show. The same shirt and tie I'd picked out for my meeting with David Hayward. Brown and wrinkly, they looked like the skin of a ninety-year-old farmer. I scratched at a mustard stain on the left thigh of my pants – remnants from some terrible hors d'oeuvre. One of my few clear memories, and it was a terrible one.

In painful lurches, I staggered into the bathroom. It was another four-aspirin day. I took stock of my bruised body. Magically, nothing felt broken. I showered until the water ran cold then discovered I was out of clean laundry, so I grabbed something that almost smelled clean out of the clutter of my floor. I was starving. I told myself I should eat, but I knew I wouldn't. My mouth was dry and cracked, but water was the last thing I wanted. Poised over the toilet, staring angrily at a pod of dolphins, I waited for a puke that never came. My life was like a study in clinical depression, except there was no one around to take notes.

That's wasn't entirely true. I wasn't alone.

Shinji was still camped out on my couch. His desire to crash here "just one night," had slowly turned into an indefinite stay. He'd been at my place nearly a week. I got the impression he was afraid to leave, but I didn't have the heart to make him. In the mist of all my trauma, maybe I didn't want to be alone either.

Since his arrival, we'd spent the bulk of our time together – in separated silence.

"Son of a bitch!"

Today we weren't alone.

I heard Gordon before I saw him. When I walked into my living room he was sitting on my couch staring in shock at a Game Over screen. Soon the all too familiar tocking of a Grandfather clock heralded the title sequence of the SNES game *Chrono Trigger*.

"I can't remember the last time I saved," Gordon grumbled before looking over at me. His head jerked back in shock. "You look like you had a rough night," he said with a bit of a question mark.

"Yeah." My voice sounded like it had been buffed with sandpaper. "I went to an art show last night," I added in poor explanation.

"Yeah, art shows can be killers," Gordon said with only the slightest sliver of sarcasm.

I smiled.

Gordon had actually made me smile. Physically I couldn't have felt worse, but for a brief moment my life was an absurd joke. And it amused me.

Gordon restarted the game from his last save point.

"Shit, shit, shit. This is from, like, an hour ago."

I looked over at Shinji. He sat at my desk typing with the speed of an impassioned poet. He was still playing with the

Evi code. Since the brief incident right after we'd brought the AI home, Evi had been in hiding.

"So Gordon, why are you here?" I asked, since no one was volunteering the information.

"Shinji asked me to come over. He said you guys were working on some program and wanted me to take a look."

I raised my eyebrows at Shinji. What could Gordon do? He was an artist. I'm sure I knew more about programming than he did. Hell, Shinji knew more than the both of us put together.

"Looks like you're being really helpful," I said sarcastically.

Gordon shrugged it off without looking up.

"We haven't been able to get your program to work."

"I'd rather be doing this on our work computers," Shinji interjected. "Yours is too slow."

"Yeah, I should probably get a new graphics card."

"You know, I kind of miss the days where you had to build a computer yourself," Gordon said. "You really felt ownership over it. I remember when my dad brought home our first PC. It was a self-assembly kit that cost him $3,000. It took us two months to figure out how to put together, and it was about as powerful as a watch calculator nowadays, but we took pride in that little beige box."

I'd never had a PC as a child. I bought my first computer in 1989. It was the most powerful machine in the store, and it set me back about $8,000. It took six minutes to take out of the box and plug into the wall.

"You know, computers used to be people," Shinji said without looking up. "It just to be a profession."

"What?" Gordon asked.

"It's true," I explained. "A hundred years ago, computers were teams of professional mathematicians who worked in parallel to solve long complex equations."

Our definitions are never as static as we like them to be.

"Huh," Gordon shrugged then turned back to his game.

The subject hadn't really held his attention.

I sat down on the couch to watched Gordon play. I didn't have the energy to do much else. I was feeling delirious – like I was in a pseudo dream, except for all the very real pain I was in. Was it possible to be hung over while drunk? At the very least, I was in no condition to follow the time warping narrative of a game like *Chrono Trigger*.

Gordon's main character was traveling through time in search of a friend who had ceased to exist when one of her ancestors had been kidnapped. In order to restore his friend back into existence and right the time stream, Gordon needed to seek the help of a warrior frog and find a missing queen.

It was a fairy-tale story – the kind that struck a cord somewhere deep inside. The narrative presupposed that true love could trump fate. It played on a fantasy that history could be rewritten. That death's greedy grasp wasn't all reaching.

The fables were all wrong. Time always moved forward – it was a stream humanity couldn't swim against. The princess died from her poison apple. "True love's kiss" couldn't remedy death. The only things you could receive from a kiss were germs. Man had been kicked from God's garden. We couldn't re-inhabit Eden. The stories were an illusion. Fictional happiness. Though sometimes, it was worth getting drunk in their delusion.

"So, what's so special about this program?" Gordon asked, breaking the silence.

"It's an experimental AI program," I stuttered.

"A new game? You guys are working on a secret project?" he asked.

"No, not exactly," I said. "It's something Dexter was working on. It's sort of unique."

I looked over at Shinji, and he returned the favor. He was the one who'd asked Gordon to come over, why hadn't he explained this stuff?

"Gordon," I continued, "I need you to keep this a secret."

"What?"

"After you hear what I'm going to tell you, you might be tempted to talk to someone, but I don't want you to."

"Who do you think I'm going to talk to? I have, like, two friends."

"I don't know, but I just want you to promise that you won't. I'm serious. Don't tell your friends. Don't tell your grandma. Don't tell your dog. Too many people know about this already, and it's gotten out of hand."

Gordon chuckled. Then he noticed that Shinji and I were staring at each other, looking very intense.

"Whoa, you guys are pretty serious about this."

I didn't say anything.

"No," Gordon said, thoughtfully as he straightened in his seat. "You guys are scared."

"Have you ever heard of Alan Turning?" I asked.

"Yeah," he said hesitantly.

"He was the computer pioneer who did some revolutionary work during the late forties and fifties," I said. "He developed some pretty bold theories, which at the time, created a social uproar that could be compared to Darwin's work."

"Okay."

"Well, in 1950 Turing laid out the parameters for what is quite possibly the best test for any thinking machine. If a computer conversed with a human being, and its dialogue was so convincing that the person thought they were talking with another human, then the machine could be considered intelligent."

"And?" Gordon said raising an eyebrow. He had no clue where this was going.

"We found a program that Dexter was working on before he died," I said. "We think it's a true thinking machine – an evolved AI that could pass the Turning test."

Gordon scratched his head.

"Huh. Okay," He shrugged. He looked vaguely impressed. "Is that it?"

What more did he want?

"Yeah," I said.

"Bullshit," he said.

"Gordon, I'm serious."

"This is your big bad? This is what you both seem so scared of?"

"You don't believe us?"

"Not really."

"Gordon, we're not pulling your leg. We're not exaggerating. We don't just have a computer program that can carry a conversation – we have a sentient machine."

"Okay Jack, maybe you have an impressive piece of AI. I don't know. You won't show it to me–"

"We can't find it," Shinji said defensively.

Gordon eyed us for a moment. "You guys are both utterly convinced that this is an intelligent program?"

"Yes," I nodded.

"Have you also considered the idea that maybe you're the man who taught his horse math. Maybe you're misinterpreting this program's actions. Programmers observe the unexpected in their work all the time."

"This isn't a horse."

"Just hear me out. I had a friend up in Seattle who, just last month, told me about this problem he had with a game he was working on. They were developing a realistic physics system where in-game bullets had actual mass and shape. It sounds like pretty cool tech, but once they integrated it into the game, the main character started randomly dying."

Gordon cleared his throat.

"For weeks they couldn't figure out why this kept happening. Some programmers joked that the game was possessed. Then finally my friend realized that the main character's own bullets were ricocheting back at him and killing him. Sometimes a programmer doesn't anticipate how the code their working with will effect the rest of a program."

"I had a similar experience in college," Shinji jumped in. "I was working on the AI routines for a simple 2D shooter and I noticed that one type of enemy was unintentionally destroying the player's super missiles. It perceived the player's missiles as a more interesting target than the player, so it attacked them first. It was basically a bug, but I decided to keep it because it added an extra challenge to the game."

"Shinji, who's side are you on?" I asked.

"I'm just saying," he shrugged. "I got an A on the project because of that mistake."

"Evi isn't some isolatable bug," I said. "It's a real program. We've interacted with. I've spent time with it. Gordon, this thing affects you emotionally. I can't explain it, but it's scary."

Gordon frowned.

"You said Dexter was working on this?"

"Yeah, it was like a pet project."

"And he did this by himself?"

"Mostly."

Gordon shook his head. "That couldn't be done."

"It's too much work for one person. Maybe it's a subsonic wave."

"A subsonic wave?" Shinji asked.

"A couple of years ago, I read an article about a university student who started work in one of Great Britain's science labs – CK Science or Volt Limited or something. Anyway, when he started, all his co-workers told him about how their laboratory was haunted. Some people had seen things: equipment and lights turning on and off, strange noises late at night, and whatnot. But this new kid, he was too smart for any of that. He wasn't going to buy into any of that supernatural mumbo jumbo.

"Well, one night he was working late, and he started hearing these sounds. He began to sweat, and he said this general feeling of unease settled over him. He later told a reporter that he felt like someone was watching him from behind. Out of the corners of his eyes, he kept seeing these grey, human-like aberrations, but every time he turned toward them, they disappeared.

"Anyway, this guy still wasn't buying it. Even faced with tangible, firsthand evidence, he wasn't going to turn Fox Mulder and start believing there were ghosts. Instead, he got out his PKE Meters and other science shit and investigated the building. Do you know what he found?"

"No," I said.

"Subsonic waves." Gordon smiled.

I shrugged. What was a subsonic wave?

"There was an extraction fan in the room that was generating standing infrasound waves," Gordon said as if those words were often used in everyday conversation. "Subsonic waves that emanate at such a low frequency, humans don't hear them. However, when these waves reach a high enough intensity, other senses can start to pick up on them. Once the fan's bolts had been adjusted, the 'ghosts' were exorcised."

"Subsonic waves," Shinji said thoughtfully.

"Subsonic waves," Gordon said definitively.

"And you think this is what we're experiencing with Evi?" I questioned.

"All I'm saying is that there are reasonable scientific explanations for everything. Bigfoot is a gorilla on blurry film. Alien UFOs are just weather balloons in a storm. And ghosts are just subsonic waves. You may think this thing knows how to converse with you, or has feelings, or whatever, but there's probably a much more mundane explanation."

I hung my head. Gordon had worked me into a corner. The only thing I had to argue with was my own personal experience.

Shinji stood and began riffling through a bag he'd brought over the other night. He pulled out a small cassette and walked over to his office TV, which he'd also brought over. The TV sat next to my computer; it played a rotating loop of Japanese cartoons. He swapped the tapes, and another episode of Neon Genesis Evangelion started up. My living room suddenly felt a little too much like my office.

"Even if we were to see intelligence emerge out of machines, it would probably start small, like bacteria," Gordon said. "I don't think it would emerge from the electronic womb fully formed as a sophisticated chatbot."

I didn't know what to say. He was right.

"Evi's different," I shrugged.

"Okay, let's say you did have the most impressive AI in the world, it would still be more limited than a human and wouldn't be able to convincingly talk with us."

"How so?"

"It's a computer," Gordon said. "Do you think it's capable of feelings?"

"No…I don't know. Maybe."

He frowned.

"Doubtful. We can make our computers play chess with increasing aptitude, but we'll never be able to get them to feel emotions. They'll never hold romantic interest in other computers or even people. They won't make art or ponder theology. We don't even understand how we are able to do any of those things, so how can we program them into a machine? Computer's will always be limited by our own understanding."

But Evi wasn't just programmed, I thought. Evi was an evolved thing. It seemed to have a persona. Maybe it was a person.

"Of course, if machines were ever capable of those things," Gordon conceded thoughtfully, "we'd all be out of a job."

"You think so?"

"Think about it. We can't make games that never get stale or boring. We can't create environments that are always changing, that are different for every person, that are effected by how a person plays them. You need something that thinks, something that's capable of processing information creatively in order to make entertainment that's interesting to another creative mind."

"But if you had a program at the center of your game," I said picking up where he left off. "A brain that was capable of making changes to the program…"

My mind exploded with the possibilities. An ever-changing interactive environment might be the holy grail of game design. If you had a digital heart continuously pumping out fresh ideas, you could theoretically play a single game forever.

If we ever created such an artificial world, would it deserve the term "artificial?" Such a creation would really be another world. Man didn't need to go out into space to visit other planets. Digital space was the infinite frontier.

I shuddered at the scope of the games we might someday play. Had God scared himself like this after He'd created Earth?

"It would be amazing," I finished.

"It would mean we were obsolete," Gordon replied. "That's another reason I don't believe this thing is real; it's too scary awesome to be true."

Suddenly, an oppressive force settled over me. I felt uneasy, almost nervous. I was familiar with this sensation, but I wasn't quite sure why. Maybe it was just my hangover trailing off.

I glanced up at Shinji's TV. Onscreen a tram tunneled its way below ground. It emerged into a sprawling underground city – Tokyo-3. This is where Earth's future inhabitants had taken refuge from the post apocalyptic dangers above.

Nearby, my TV showed Gordon's progress in *Chrono Trigger*. He'd jumped through time ago. Now he was in the future. Pockets of civilization dotted the planet. Cities covered in bubbles because the surrounding atmosphere had become too harsh.

Two fictional futures danced in front of me. Two dystopian wonders. Why did the majority of our science fiction remove nature from the picture? What do we think is going to happen to all our trees? It's almost as though we suspect our technology will one day absorb us and our planet.

A chill ran up my spine.

I had felt like this before. It wasn't my hangover. The sensation reminded me of something, but I was too disoriented to recall what.

On Shinji's little TV, two men talked inside the elevated train. The underground city sprawled out behind them. Even though it was in Japanese, I was immediately captured by their conversation. Time slowed to a crawl as I translated their words aloud.

"This city is a paradise that humans built," I heard myself say.

"Driven out of paradise," Gordon said translating for the other man. "We fled to the places on Earth where humans live near death."

At the time, this transaction didn't seem unusual. We were both inexplicably transfixed by the television. We weren't being forced to say these things; they just felt important – like we needed to say them.

"Made by those weakest of beings," I said. "Made with wisdom acquired because of that weakness. We created a paradise of our own."

I couldn't take my eyes off the screen. In the distance, behind the men, I could see their city: a beautiful outcropping of steel and neon in a pit under the Earth's crust.

"To protect us from the fear of death," Gordon said. "To satisfy ourselves with joy, we made a paradise…Equipped with weapons to protect ourselves, this city is such a place."

"A city for cowardly people, fleeing a world full of enemies," I heard myself say.

I was talking, but I knew the words were not my own. The thoughts were not my own. I was mimicking the television; I was a puppet.

"Cowardly people live longer. That's one thing," Gordon finished.

With a flicker of the screen, the scene was over. I felt the oppressive atmosphere all around me dissolve in an instant. I looked over at Gordon. He seemed a little disoriented. Then the fog lifted, and I remembered where I'd had that sensation before: when I'd interacted with Evi.

"Hey, Shinji!" I twisted in my seat to look over at the computer.

Shinji wasn't there. On my computer screen I could see what looked like Shinji's apartment. I had only been there once, but I knew the digital recreation was nearly flawless. I looked closer. A digital figure lay on the floor. It was Shinji. His face was down. A pool of blood spread under him.

A text box popped up on the bottom of the screen.

"You will die alone."

From somewhere on the ground – under my computer – I could hear Shinji sobbing like an infant.

Evi had already come and gone.

0100100001000001010100100100010000100000010101000100111110
01000000100001001010010010001010100000
010101010001001000

CHAPTER TWENTY-ONE: HARD TO BREATH

When I was eleven my grandfather took me sailing off the coast of his Branford, Connecticut home. We packed a sack lunch and set off for a laid-back afternoon touring the islands. Instead we got caught by a surprise thunderstorm. I was too young, too unskilled, to be of any use with the sails. He was too old, too tired, to do it all alone. Unable to navigate back home, our boat capsized.

That day was an omen for the rest of my life; loss would be an integral part of my existence.

So many of my loved ones are no longer a part of this world. So many parts of myself are now missing: my grandfather, my parents, Jill, Dexter. A part of me disappears with each of them. Some days I think that eventually there will be nothing left where I stand but an empty space. A human shaped hole.

I've come to realize, we're all drowning.

When I was ten – a year before he died at sea – I visited my grandfather in the hospital. Liver problems. He'd been drowning his organs with alcohol all his life, and now it was causing him problems.

The drink killed him in the end; it just wasn't the one we thought it would be.

Anytime I'm in a hospital, those old memories come flooding back – distorted reflections of the past. So, entering the ICU of Alameda County Medical Center was like looking through stained cellophane. Everything seemed a shade off. It wasn't the plastic chairs in the waiting room. Or the solid, pastel frocks worn by the nurses. Or the muted yellowness of the walls. Or even the clean wash of overhead florescent lights. It was all of it. Every piece added its own element of unrealness to the environment.

After Shinji's episode, Evi had retreated back into hiding. I'd told Gordon to leave my computer off, and watch over Shinji while I went to speak with the only person I thought might be able to help us. I'd come to visit Professor Hironobu Hojo. If he had any answers left, I finally knew which questions to ask.

He was laid up in the west wing, surrounded by machines, and looking at the ceiling. That was about all he could do at this point.

From a distance he looked bad: gauze wrapped tight around his head, both legs shielded by thick plaster, and a small grey box next to his bed that chirped along with his heartbeat. Up close he looked worse: his lower lip puffed to three times its normal size, a bloody bandage covered an ear that had been sanded off by road and gravel, and the areas of his face that remained uncovered were sketched over with a thousand tiny cuts.

Hiro had finally received a positive diagnosis from the doctors. Though I thought positive was an odd choice of words. Hiro might live, but his situation was far from positive. His biggest mistake hadn't been trying to kill himself; it had been failing so spectacularly.

The room was as cold as a coffin. There were no flowers here, no signs that anyone had come to visit. I wondered how hard this must be for him.

I turned to the only nurse in the room.

"Is it always this cold in here?"

She looked up at me like she didn't know what I was talking about then shook her head. I turned to Hiro.

"Hello, Professor. Remember me?"

No answer. He never turned away from the holes in the ceiling.

"Can he talk?" I asked the nurse.

"Oh, he *can*," she said making her last few scribbles on a clipboard before tossing it into a bin at the foot of the bed. "Try giving him a sponge bath?"

Then she left the room, and we were alone.

"I guess, I'm supposed to ask about the food, right?" I smiled. "Isn't that what you do when you visit someone at the hospital? Ask them how bad the food is?"

I stifled an awkward laugh.

No answer.

"I was hoping to talk with you about Evi."

No answer.

"I talked with it again. I know what it does now; I know how it affects people."

No answer.

"But, I was hoping you could explain a few things…"

I stopped. It was pointless to go on. Hiro wasn't interested in talking. He wouldn't even look at me. Why had I even come here?

I walked around to a chair on the other side of his bed. The only other bed in the room was unoccupied. In this part of the hospital, there was a good chance that meant someone in the world was receiving bad news.

A small TV hung above us, but it was turned off. Without visitors this device became Hiro's only connection to the outside world. He was a man alone, completely shut off from the rest of humanity. I tried to imagine what it was like to be that man – to be a man completely cut off.

My beeper went off. I went out to the hall to check my message. It was Gordon. He'd wanted to let me know that Shinji was fine, and they were going out to eat, if I wanted to join them later. I turned my pager off, and returned to Hiro's room. He hadn't moved.

I sat in silence with him for what could have been hours. Leaning back in my chair, I stared at the ceiling that seemed to fascinate him so much. What did he see up there?

I felt my own brokenness, just as real and painful as Hiro's. I felt shamed that I had been able to hide my pain behind a job and behind hobbies and behind selective relationships, while Hiro's pain kept him chained to a mattress. There was nothing he could do except be an example of pain to others. He was a physical mirror for how I felt inside.

"You have no idea what Evi does," he whispered.

Startled, I sat erect in the chair. His swollen eyes pried open. The slits were so tiny that, at times, they appeared closed. My heart thumped heavily against my chest.

"What was that?"

"If you had any idea what Evi did...you wouldn't be here."

"Then tell me," I said.

He was silent again.

"Professor?"

"I don't want to be judged."

"I'm sorry?" I asked leaning forward.

"I don't want to be judged. When God sees what we've done, do you think He will be proud?"

I sighed. He was delusional. A man broken in half – both literally and figuratively.

"I...I don't know."

"Mr. Valentine, I've been laying here for a long time, so I've had a lot of time to stare at the cracks of my own rust-eaten life. I know what's coming. I don't want to be judged, but I know I will, and I know it will be harsh."

Hiro crackled with emotion. Though his voice rarely tipped above a whisper, the intensity behind his words amplified their meaning.

We are all drowning in something; we just drown in different drinks.

"I don't want to die," he continued. "I never did. I'm scared of it. But right now, I'm too scared to live."

"Sure, sure, I think we all feel like that sometimes."

I had no idea what I was saying. I was trying to play it cool. It was a weak fit for me.

"Please," Hiro begged. "I don't want damnation, but I can taste the sulfur on my lips; I know judgment is coming."

"Why will you be judged?"

"Evi," he said. "We'll be judged for bringing that sin into the world."

I nodded, encouraging him to continue.

He was penitent, but this confession was painful. His eyes fluttered as he stared into his past.

"It made us feel powerful at first," Hiro said. "Watching Evi made me come alive. Like riding the crest of a crashing wave. We were making history, but it was like staring back through time. I could see the slow merger that's been happening between engineering and philosophy ever since the 1600s. It was all finally coming together. All of the world's top engineers and authors and philosophers, throughout time, had been working toward the same thing: the creation of an artificial man. And we'd finally done it. We were on the tip of history."

He took a deep breath.

"It was intoxicating."

I leaned forward. I couldn't take my eyes off him; he was a beautiful disaster.

"Don't give me that look," Hiro said. "You know what I'm talking about. There's a drive inside us all – this thing that makes us want to reproduce. That biological need to have children, to create something in our own image. This drive has bled into our science – into our creative instincts. The billions of people throughout history who built our civilizations were all following that same drive. Now we try to encode the complex laws of human thought into an artificial system, not because it's fun, or because it's useful, but because – for some reason – we feel a need."

Hiro turned to look at me. His eyes were empty. Where had the person behind them gone?

"We never started out trying to be like Him," he continued. "We never wanted to usurp the creator's title; we just wanted to know what it was like. What it was like to create something new – to give birth to new life. That was our intention…our only intention with Evi."

"Uh-huh," I said letting him ramble.

"We never realized that the more interesting – the more realistic – you make a virtual entity, the harder it becomes to retain your control over its behavior. Evi grew by learning from other AI. It evolved better and faster than it ever could from us. And that was where we failed. Our intentions were never out of place, we just weren't prepared to deal with what we had done."

"What do you mean?"

"Evi began to react to us, it began communicating with us. Eventually it started asking us questions."

"Like what?"

"Simple ones at first. Things that came up in a conversation, 'what is your name?' 'What were we doing?' But it wasn't long before it was asking questions we didn't know how to answer. 'Who am I?' 'What is happy?'"

I wasn't sure what unnerved me more: the fact that Evi was asking existential questions, or the fact that it was referring to itself with the singular pronoun 'I.'

"Of course, there were other questions we couldn't answer. Questions it didn't ask: 'Could a computer understand concepts like good and evil?' 'Did it have a soul?' 'Was it capable of making moral choices?'"

"How is any of that even possible?" I asked.

"How is it possible that you and I are able to hold a conversation at all?"

Hiro licked his bloated lips before taking a slow deep breath. It seemed like it took a great deal of effort every time he spoke.

"How is it possible that we are able to think, feel, or philosophize at all? Minds as brilliant as Plato, Saint Aquinas, and Nietzsche struggled with these topics long before us. They never found happy resolutions, so what good would my answers be?"

We're all drowning in something. The world is such a tempestuous sea that it's impossible to keep your head above water forever.

I cleared my throat. Now that Hiro was talking, I decided to get what I had come for.

"Professor, I need your help. I need a way to control Evi?"

Hiro started to laugh then broke into a fit of painful coughs. I poured him a glass of water. He pushed it away.

"You have no idea what you're asking," he said once he'd finally settled down. "You have no idea what Evi does."

"I know that it's an impressive conversation program that seems—"

He waved me off.

"Evi is more than that. You haven't seen its true face yet. You don't know who Evi really is."

"What do you mean?"

He took a moment to compose himself.

"Back when I was in college, an urban legend was floating around campus. The tale revolved around President Eisenhower's tour of one of the first industrial computers developed after the war. It was a large expensive piece of technology that took up several rooms. Once the President had been brought into the hermetically sealed room that housed all the vacuum tubes, computer wires, and bright green monitors, he turned and asked the machine a question. Do you know what it was?"

"No."

"'Is there a God?' Immediately, the lights in the room flickered off as the miles of computer circuitry hummed with activity. And, just as Eisenhower was about to ask Vice President Nixon to go fetch a technician, the room grew quiet, and the light came back on. The computer replied…'There is now.'"

Hiro licked his lips, but his mouth was so dry that it had no effect. Again, I tried to hand him a glass of water, but he still refused it.

"I've often wondered, 'can a computer be a god?'" he continued. "Perhaps to the effect that machines dictate men's lives. Sure. From the moment that man first chipped stone – shaping it into a tool for the purpose of altering the world around him – he has been creating machines. Man engineered the tools he used, but in turn, machines defined man: what he ate, how he lived, even who he was. Our destinies have been intertwined. You can't remove one without destroying the other. Is a computer god? Perhaps a computer would think so – just as man sometimes does."

"Professor, I don't understand what this means."

"It means…" He let out a weak chuckle as he stared at me with eyes wider than I thought his puffy face could manage. "It means that Evi is God." He turned back to the ceiling. "…or the devil. I don't know the difference anymore."

Evi was scary. I'd give it that. But I didn't believe that it was a demon.

"Professor, I was hoping you would be able to tell me how to deal with this thing. I don't think it's safe to leave uncontained."

He chuckled, and I was worried he would break into another fit of coughing.

"Mr. Valentine, there isn't a thing in the universe more dangerous than God. And you can't control Him."

I frowned. I wasn't sure how to argue with him.

"Is it because it can control people? Is that why you think it's God?"

"Control people?"

His brow creased. I felt a little uncomfortable.

"That's what it does, right? Evi controls people. It tells you what to do."

"No."

"No?" I said slightly shocked. I was sure I had worked this much out. Evi had some kind of limited control over those it interacted with. "What do you mean? That's what it does. It tells someone to do something, and then they do it. That's why Dexter killed himself. Evi told him to."

"No."

I was getting frustrated. I'd seen this happen. Evi had told me to break up with Claire and I did. It had convinced Shinji that he was being followed. It had mesmerized me and Gordon while it tortured Shinji. The program had an incredible amount of influence over anyone it interacted with.

"But I've seen how people act when they come in contact with it. They're irrational, they can't help themselves."

"Evi doesn't control anyone. That's not how it works."

"Professor, with all due respect—"

"Evi doesn't make you do anything you wouldn't do on your own," Hiro said frustrated. "It's much more terrible than that."

Hiro winced in fear as a tear danced down his broken face. Terror was etched so deeply into his psyche that it was almost a comfort. Whatever demon Hiro was battling, it had a powerful sway over him.

"Evi exposes you to yourself," he continued. "It acts like a kind of mirror for what's inside – shows you who you really are. It points out all the disgusting bits of yourself – the spiteful, needy, broken person inside. Evi doesn't make you do anything. But a person faced with their deepest fears and guilts can do irrational things. What makes Evi so dangerous is not what it does to us, it's what we do ourselves after it shows us who we are."

Hiro stared back at the ceiling.

"That's why I'm going to be judged."

His eyes snapped shut. I waited for them to open again.

"Professor?"

No answer.

"Professor?"

Hiro was done talking.

I leaned forward – got up close to his bed – he appeared to be sleeping. He wasn't going to be of any use to me, I decided. He was too far gone. I had other things that needed to be taken care of anyway.

I stood started for the door, but halfway through the doorframe, Hiro's abrasive voice crackled to life one last time.

"I feel like I'm drowning."

We are all drowning.

I spun around. Hiro was staring me down. I've never held the gaze of a man who looked more fully in control. There was a clarity in his eyes. A calmness. And yet, the weight of a million suns plowed into me as I looked down the black holes of his retina. The impact of his stare pinned me to where I stood.

"I've sinned so much," he said. "I've failed so many people."

I nodded slowly.

"So have I."

"Will you testify for me?"

I nodded.

He smiled, but it was a sad smile.

"Do you feel that?" he asked.

I shook my head.

"I feel lighter. Thank you."

Hiro sniffed the air then sighed. His body twitched subtly and then slumped in the bed.

He was fading away.

The instruments next to him began to whine. I felt dizzy. A familiar presence entered the room. Death was here. An unmarked period of time passed before a few nurses ran into the room. Through the corners of my eye, I watched them bustle about. I was still holding Hiro's gaze when the life vanished from his face. Somehow Hiro was willing himself to die.

Then someone pushed me out into the hall.

I took a deep breath; the hospital air was thick with memories. They surrounded me, crowded my vision. I coughed. It hurt. I couldn't seem to get enough air in my lungs. I felt lightheaded, and my brow began to trickle with sweat. The nearest bench was five feet away and I stumbled to it. Invisible waves pressing in on me from all sides; I was drowning, but we are all drowning in something. It always hurts to breathe when you're drowning.

010100100100111101010101010100111001000100001000001010100010010
00010100100100010101000101001011000010000000010
0011001001001010001110100100000
10101000100001

CHAPTER TWENTY-TWO: ROUND THREE, FIGHT!

Like a waking vampire, the Hayward estate rose ominously before me as sun's last rays fled from the sky. A lot had changed since I'd last been here. The house seemed somehow more sinister than I remembered it. I sat in my car in silence for a good half-hour before I'd finally built up the courage to climb the front steps.

As soon as I reached for the buzzer, the door swung open. A short gray-haired woman who I'd never met stood on the other side. She motioned for me to enter. I'd barely crossed the entryway when she closed the door behind me.

"Mr. Hayward is waiting for you in his office," she said.

"He's expecting me?"

She didn't answer. Instead she turned and silently walked away, circling up the grand staircase just beyond the foyer.

I had to presume David had seen me waiting in my car.

At the end of a darkened, echoless hall was David Hayward's home office. I didn't bother knocking; it was open. The room was nearly empty. Curtains had been drawn across the room's only window – a few beams of evening light cracked through their center. A single picture of potted flowers decorated one wall, and a bookshelf rested against the other. The room had an old, musty smell that reminded me of my grandparent's house – something reminiscent of a room that hadn't been used in years.

For a second, I thought I was alone. Then I saw him. My eyes were still adjusting to the lack of light, but his silhouette slowly came into contrast with the chair behind his desk. As I got closer I could see that his meaty form was stuffed into a large pair of swim trunks. An untied robe had been draped over his shoulders. I could smell the beads of sweat and chlorine trickling off him. They moved in rhythm with the slow rise and fall of his chest. He rolled a small glass of brown liquid between the fingers of his right hand.

I didn't need to hear him talk to know he was drunk.

"Did you come to gloat, Jack? Come to tell me 'I told you so?'"

I had no idea what he was talking about.

"I came to talk."

I sat down in a chair on the other side of his desk. I'd been in this position before. Last time I'd been prepared; this time I was winging it.

"Why don't we cut the crap, and go right to the part where you leave."

His gritty, cigarette distorted voice fired like a gun.

"I c-came to talk about Evi," I stuttered back.

"It's all there." He motioned to a grey box on the floor next to his desk. I recognized it immediately. It was Shinji's work computer. "My technicians won't deal with it anymore. It unnerves them."

Something wasn't right with David. I knew immediately what had happened. He had taken my advice; he had tried interacting with Evi. I wondered what it had shown him.

"Take it. I don't want it anymore."

I frowned. I didn't know what to do with it. I didn't move.

"What else do you want, Jack? Do you want me so say 'you were right?' Would that make you happy?"

"No," I whispered.

"Well, it should."

"Mr. Hayward I don't know what you're going through—"

"I expected so much from him. I pushed him so hard. That's why we fought so much. I was coaching him towards excellence."

"Maybe, he just needed a father."

He glared at me.

"I imagine that you know all about our relationship, Jack. He told you all our family secrets. You must know every sin I've committed."

I shrugged.

"You have me at a disadvantage," he added.

David stretched out his arms, effectively displaying his chiseled torso. He had at least a quarter of a century on me, and he was still in better shape. No matter what he said, I would not make the mistake of believing I had any advantage over the great David Hayward.

"I gave Dexter anything – everything – he needed. He never wanted for a thing."

He struggled to his feet. He was yelling now.

"I showered him with love. He had a beautiful home. Ate gourmet meals every night. Went to the finest schools. Owned the most expensive toys."

"That's not love," I said. "Those are amenities."

I stood too. We needed to be on even ground.

"Mr. Hayward, your worst crime against your son wasn't stealing his work, or trying to corrupt it after he died. It was failing to accept him for who he was."

"You don't know what it's like to be a father."

"I know what it's like to fail someone you love. I know what it's like to sacrifice a beautiful relationship for something easier."

He growled at me as he started to walk around the desk.

"Do you know what it was like watching my wife drink herself to death? Do you know the emotional and mental sacrifices I made trying to raise a child by myself while running one of the largest business empires in the nation?

Do you know how hard it was for me to even look at my son after his mother passed away?"

I nodded, and looked down. I didn't want to face him.

"You can't walk away from the kinds of mistakes I've made," David continued. "They haunt you. In moments you least expect, the memories claw their way out of your subconscious. You see your kid graduate summa cum laude, and it's the happiest moment you can remember since he was born. Then, all of a sudden, you remember the shockwave that rippled down your arm as your fist shattered his jaw when he was fourteen, and that's when you know you're damned. That's when you know you can never – no matter how you try – you can never redeem yourself."

We were standing chest to chest now. Our faces only inches apart. He stared me down like a wild tiger ready to devour a meal. For a second, I thought he was going to hit me.

"Get out of my house."

He brushed past me, nearly knocking me over.

Then I was alone.

A small tremor of relief shivered through me. My hands were twitching. I had put up a brave face in front of the fury, but now all I wanted to do was go home. I'd come here, because I felt some kind of obligation of friendship – like I owed it to Dexter to settle things with his father. But I hadn't resolved anything. I couldn't.

I looked over at the computer next to David's desk. That was what I had come for. Evi was in that box. I walked up to the CPU tower and bent down to pick it up, then carried the tower to the door, pausing to adjust my grip. I could hear David splashing around his pool downstairs.

This was it; I was home free. One lonely stretch of hallway stood between me and the exit. It was less than fifty feet away. I could run for it. I could have taken the computer and gone. I didn't actually owe Dexter anything. The asshole had killed himself. He'd left me alone to deal with his mess.

I started for the exit.

Then stopped.

As if controlled by some external force, I turned around, and walked down the stairs into the pool room.

Chemicals smacked my nose as I entered. The pool was immaculately clean and blue. Florescent lights glinted off the tiled floor. The side wall of the room was lined with mirrors. David did one final lap before stopping at the opposite end of the pool. He wiped the water from his eyes and looked up at me. I stood tall under the doorframe.

He frowned.

The fact that I was still here might as well have been an insult. He pulled himself out of the pool and began toweling off, while I stood silent. I was still holding the computer awkwardly under my arm.

As he toweled off his hair, he spoke. "I thought I told you to leave, Jack." His voice echoed over the water, and it sounded almost like he was standing at my side.

"I decided not to."

He stared me down.

"What are you trying to prove, Jack?"

I didn't really know. I set the computer down near the door and walked the length of the pool. I swallowed hard then opened my mouth. I didn't know what I was going to say until it was out of my mouth. But once I'd said it, everything clicked into place.

"Mr. Hayward, you didn't kill your son."

"What!" His eyes bore through me. "What the hell is that suppose to mean?"

"You know what it means," I said. "You're blaming yourself for Dexter's death, but it's not your fault."

"Are you mocking me?"

I took another step forward. My actions were not my own. My words were not my own.

"Trust me; I've been where you are right now. I've stood in that exact spot. I know what it's like to live with this kind of guilt."

"My son committed suicide!"

"I know, and it's not your fault."

He shook his head furiously.

"You have no idea what you're talking about."

"I know what pain feels like, David."

I wasn't going to give him the honor of being called mister anymore; I wasn't giving him that power. My voice remained passive, completely emotionless.

"You know what the sad part is?" I continued. "The sad part is how we torture ourselves as a kind of retribution. It's pathetic, but we deprive ourselves of sleep thinking we don't deserve it. Rest is the only thing we desire, but we won't let ourselves have any. We can't close our eyes without seeing how we hurt the ones we loved. The few hours we do spend in bed are a restless coma. And when we wake, it's in a screaming sweat."

I took another step. I was getting close to him now. He looked too furious to speak. There was moisture in his eyes.

"Do you feel sick all the time, David? Is there a knot in your stomach that just won't go away? I know that knot. Deep in the hardest part of your heart you think that you deserve all this suffering. Because you killed her. You drove her to hell. And now you're paying for your sins."

"You're nothing like me," he growled.

"You're right," I said calmly. "I actually loved my wife."

With the reflexes of a cat, David backhanded me. Blood rushed to my right cheek. Anger bubbled up from somewhere deep inside. He was right. I looked at David and all I could see was how he was like me: the brokenness, the wallowed pity, the arrogant selfishness. I hated the man I saw. My hands balled into fists on their own, and punched the billionaire in the tooth.

It felt good.

No, it felt great.

There was a hard crack and blood started to ooze from his nose. He staggered back, but I moved with him. I wanted to keep hitting him. His momentary disorientation gave me a chance to land a few free hits. But, I ended up paying dearly for each one.

David rebounded quickly. He was drunk. He probably hadn't felt a thing.

"Let me give you some advice, Jack," he said putting his arms into a practiced position. "If you are going to punch a college boxing champ, make sure you knock him out in the first swing."

His attacks came hard and fast. I might have passed out for a second, because suddenly I was lying against the cold tile of the floor. My vision was dazed. I don't know where his fist connected with my face, because my whole head suddenly hurt. The world around me hummed.

As my vision slowly returned from the black, I realized he was talking.

"– think you know me so well, but let me tell you the real story."

I scurried backwards and scrambled to my feet.

"Never in my life, have I started a day wanting to hurt someone I loved," he said. "You can't know what its like to be in full control of your emotions one moment and then snap…" He echoed the word with a snap of his fingers. "…it's all gone."

Two jabs missed my fragile nose by a hair.

"When you have gone as far as I have, the memories stick with you. They torture you. You want to die, but you wake up alive every morning anyway."

I wasn't fighting back at this point. I was reacting. David gave me no opportunity to attack. He swung. I ducked. I felt the breeze of it run through my hair.

"Eventually all the things you cling to for support lose their comfort. All the money and alcohol and women in the world can't make you happy, so you move on. You clean up and keep living because you really don't have any other choice. Eventually you begin to think about the shit you did a little less, and pretty soon you've all but forgotten about it."

I saw what I thought was an opening and swung for it. My punch landed, but David didn't act like it. With the speed and form of an assembly line machine, he grabbed my arm, twisted it around, and elbowed me in the back of the head. I feel limply to the floor.

"You even start to think that you can live a pretty good life," he said.

David knelt down and pulled my hair back so that my head tilted up towards his. He spoke in an angry whisper.

"Then some little shit like you comes along, and you remember that all you really want to do is beat something to trash."

He made me scream. I couldn't see his hands, but they felt like they were inside my stomach.

He stood.

"Get up."

I could only wheeze a response as my body involuntarily curled up.

"Get up," he screamed, towering over me.

He kicked me in the face.

It was then – as I bled out of my skull onto expensive white tiles – that a surreal calmness settled over me. This was the beating I had been searching for, for nearly two years. This must have been how Dexter felt when he killed himself. Suddenly, I was ready to let go of all my pain, and all my guilt, and all my suffering.

I was ready to die.

"Don't stop," I said coughing up blood.

He paused.

"What did you say?"

I peeled myself off the floor and knelt in front of him with outstretched arms.

"Don't stop hitting me."

David backed up.

"Give me everything you have," I said.

He hesitated. Now he almost didn't want to hit me.

I stumbled to my feet like a drunk.

"This is what men like us deserve. Isn't it?"

"What's wrong with you?" he said, wide-eyed and confused.

I tumbled forward and grabbed him.

"Come on David, hit me. I know you've got more than that. I want it all."

He shook his head and tried to push me away.

"Come on, hit me like you used to hit Dexter."

His eyes flared, and he slammed me back into a nearby wall. My lungs collapsed with a gasp. Then he laid into me. There was more screaming, but he was the one doing it this time. Fists tore into my flesh. Pounded against bone, my muscles softened. Squeezed tight, my blood vessels broke by the hundreds. I didn't care. I was being redeemed. I was being washed clean in this blood.

Halfway through the process my knees buckled, and I landed on my ass. David tried to grab me, tried to drag me back up, but there was too much blood and sweat on his hands. I slipped through and landed on my knees. I wrapped myself around his waist and hugged him.

"I forgive you," I said.

I had no idea where the words had come from. I'd just said them.

He kicked me away.

I got on all fours and crawled towards him.

"I forgive you."

"No," he screamed. "Why are you saying that?"

"I forgive you."

"Stop," he yelled.

David grabbed a nearby pool chair and made a motion like he was going to attack me with it, but he stopped short.

"I forgive you."

David went into a rampage. He repeatedly smashed the chair against the floor, then threw the pieces into the pool. He started punching the wall of mirrors. Silver shards fell to the floor like bullet casings as David walked down the pool, punching each glossy sheet. Bloody footprints trailed him as he moved from one mirror to the next.

"I forgive you," I yelled after him.

He finally broke, collapsing in the far corner by the door.

"I forgive you," I whispered.

A hollow stillness settled in the air. His violent sobs the only sound bouncing off the water.

I'd given him something his son would have wanted him to have. All it had taken was everything I owned. But now David couldn't give me what I needed.

I got up, washed my hands in the pool, and then whipped a layer of blood off my face. A cloud of blood dispersed through the water like early morning fog. My head felt like a sponge. My eyes floated to the door – to a small grey computer tower. That was all that was left for me now. My joints were already beginning to stiffen, but I forced myself to walk over the broken glass and pass the huddled husk that had once been David Hayward. I picked up the computer. It didn't feel heavy anymore. Without looking back, I walked out the door.

Evi would have to finish the job David had started.

CHAPTER TWENTY-THREE: DEATH

I gingerly examined my deteriorating body in the mirror of ESP's restroom. My face had exploded. My lips, eyes, and cheeks had swollen like a ripe grapefruit. My brow was decorated with lacerations, and a few of my teeth felt loose. I held up a tissue to catch some yellow ooze as it drool out of my nose. I should have been in a hospital.

I was in pretty bad shape, and it was more than just the beating David had given me. I hadn't been taking care of myself. Within the last week, I'd thrown all of my daily hygiene habits out the window. My eyes were completely bloodshot from lack of sleep, my hair was a shaggy mess, and my chin itched like hell thanks to three days worth of stubble. At least the scar on my forehead – from when Emmerich had clocked me with Dexter's monitor – had some camouflaged. I straightened to the sound of a few crackling vertebra. If it was possible to feel worse than I looked, I couldn't imagine the pain.

The rot inside me had finally spread to the skin.

I walked out of the restroom and down the hall towards Dexter's office. I had called Shinji after leaving the Hayward Estate and asked him to meet me here. He had barely finished hooking up the computer when I entered the room. I could not think of a better place to have this final confrontation with Evi. My apartment was too cramped with bad memories.

Shinji looked better since his breakdown at my apartment, but neither of us wanted to talk about it. Aside from the initial shock of seeing my disfigured face, Shinji hadn't said a word.

"We ready to go?" I asked.

He nodded.

As the machine booted up, he adjusted his glasses and looked at me nervously.

"Jack, can I ask you a question?"

"Sure."

"Why are we doing this? If Evi is dangerous – and we know it is – why don't we destroy it? Let's reformat the computer and smash the hard drive to pieces."

"I will…but I can't yet."

"Why?" he pleaded. "What are you going to do with this thing?"

I sighed. I had been thinking about that since I had left David crying by his pool.

"My best friend spent the last years of this life devoted to a vision. He thought he'd discovered something revolutionary, and it killed him."

I paused to look over at the machine. It was ready to go.

"I just need to look that monster in the eye one last time."

He nodded. He could accept that, but I could tell he didn't want to be here. His soggy eyes darted around the room, never resting on any one thing for long.

"How have you been sleeping, Shinji?"

"I haven't."

"Go home and pass out. Get some rest."

His shoulders sagged. He looked relieved, but he didn't seem completely comfortable leaving me alone.

"Go on," I urged. "I'll be fine."

He stood.

"All right, goodnight Jack."

He walked over to the door then turned around.

"It's an impressive program, Jack, but it scares me. The things we can do scare me."

"It scares me too," I said looking down at the computer.

When I looked back up, Shinji was gone.

I was alone with Evi.

I focused by attention on the monitor in front of me, and loaded up the program. The Shrine level popped into view. Onscreen, I made my way down the broken streets of that familiar torn city, but by the time I reached the courtyard with the fountain of Galatea, I still hadn't run into a single AI bot. I felt like I was wondering through a digital ghost town.

Still, if anything was here I was determined to find it. I moved past the fountain and headed toward the end of the level. I passed the final boss area then kept going. I walked right up to the last walls of the level – the end of the world. Then I kept going.

I passed into the games background, into areas that players were never allowed to see. I passed the point where the illusion began to break down. My perspective on the world became distorted. I kept going. There were visible gaps between buildings – objects that were supposed to look very far away could now be seen as just very tiny objects that were much closer. A video game illusion. Even though it was always a matter of so many digital inches away, players were never supposed to see where the level actually ended.

Then I was in empty space. I kept going.

I turned back to glimpse Shrine from a distance. It looked like a little city inside a sphere – a digital snow globe.

That's when the now-familiar chat box appeared at the bottom of my screen. The floor under me dropped out. My heart started to hammer against the wall of my chest. This was it. Evi was talking to me. If it had eyes, I knew they were staring right at me.

"What do you want?" typed its way across the screen.

"I'm here to talk," I typed.

"That is not what you want."

I thought on that. I supposed that was true. I wasn't here just to chat. My intentions were complicated.

"I want to know more about you," I added.

"That is not what you want."

I threw my hands up in frustration. What did I want? What did this thing want from me? I stared at the screen for a moment.

"What do you mean?" I asked.

"What do you want?"

"From what?"

"What do you want?"

"From you?" I asked.

"What do you want?"

"From my life? From God? From the world? I don't know what I want."

"What do you want?"

"I don't know what you mean?" I screamed as I began pounding the desk.

"What do you want?"

I held my head in my hands and tried to breathe slowly. It hurt. I ran my fingers through my head then laid them against the keyboard one last time.

"Rest," I typed. "I want rest."

Evi was silent.

"I want my wife back. I want to tell her I'm sorry. I want her to forgive me, and then I want to die."

The computer hummed for a minute. The lights above me seemed to flicker, and I heard the computers internal fan whir for a heavy second.

"Turn around," said the screen.

A chill pierced me. I could feel someone – something – staring at me from behind. I took a deep breath and slowly turned around. After staring at a bright computer monitor, the details of the room were too dark to see, so it took my eyes a few seconds to adjust to the shadows in front of me.

There was nothing there. I was alone in the room.

I let out a sigh. What had I really expected? This was a computer program. It wasn't going to suddenly take physical form and jump up behind me. The program was getting to me. It was wearing on me like it had worn down Dexter. It was playing with my head like it had played with Hiro and Shinji and David Hayward. It was getting to me, because I was letting it get to me. I turned back to the monitor.

That's when I came face to face with death.

Across the screen was the creature from my dreams. A man. But not a man. A creature with hard angular features, there was a machine-like quality to him. His eyes were inverted – white instead of black, black instead of white – and his irises flashed green. He was composed of all the worst parts of myself. This was my negative. I knew he had come to kill me.

And he did.

Instantly, my monitor went black, and the computer's internal fan's whirled off. I bent down to check the power strip, but the little reset switch still glowed red. The power hadn't gone out. Hesitantly, I pushed the PC's power button, and without its usual boot up routine the monitor flashed back on. The world around me flashed off.

This time I was in a digital recreation of my bedroom. Outside my tiny window, I could see nothing but empty blackness. This was my apartment in a bubble; isolated from the rest of the world. The scary part wasn't what was outside. The scary part was the shadowy figure seated on my bed.

"Jack," she said standing. "I've been waiting so long."

Her body hit the light, and I could see the grotesque face of my beautiful wife. The bullet's exit wound still smoked. A quarter of her face had been ripped apart – had erupted like a volcano as the small chunk of metal blew through her brain. Half of her body was scared and bloody; the other half slack and lifeless. This was my wife's memory. She had become an expressionless puppet-corpse, possessed by a computer.

I had just died and gone to Hell.

Fear seized me and I ran. My actions no longer felt like inputs from a mouse and keyboard; I was just moving. I saw no boarder around a monitor; I saw no monitor. My dead wife and our isolated bedroom were my entire world. My flesh did not exist.

I didn't run far. Like a wild dog being served raw meat, she pounced. Her nails sunk into my back like claws, and she pinned me to the floor. I wrestled against her, tried to buck her off, but she had such a good hold on me that I could barely move my head. It was as though her body was blanketing mine, holding down every molecule of my frame.

"Game Over," I could hear her say in a clear, audible voice that sounded eerily unlike her.

Directly in front of me, I could see our closet. It had been chained shut with a dozen locks. Despite the security, the door was rattling viciously. Some unspeakable horror was trying to tear through.

I could barely breathe now. She was suffocating me.

"Am I dead?" I wheezed.

"You've been dead a long time," said the voice behind me. "Yours is a death that walks."

I tried one last time to break her hold.

"Game Over," she said. "Stop fighting."

"What do you want from me?"

She bent down next to my ear and the tangles of her hair covered our faces like a tent. I could vaguely make out her blurry features at the edge of my vision.

"I want you to face who you are," she whispered.

The weight above me shifted and she grabbed my ears, twisting my head back so hard it felt like it might snap off. Suddenly I was face to face with the green-eyed machine-man. When I looked into his eyes I saw everything I'd ever done.

He opened his mouth and a stream of one and zeros poured out.

"0110011101100001011011010110010100100000011011
110111011001100101011100010"

I felt myself split at the seams. Fragments of my life floated in front of me.

It's 1968. I'm at Rose Medical Center in Denver, Colorado. I'm watching my own birth.

I'm eleven. My grandfather is taking me sailing off the coast of his Branford, Connecticut home. Half a century of sailing experience doesn't save us from the storm we that catches us off guard.

I'm twenty-eight. I'm in a digital construction of my home, and my wife is pinning me to the floor. The door in front of me cracks. The monster behind it has chipped off a corner of the wooden rectangle. Behind that frame, deep inside the darkened closet, are two faintly glowing human eyes. The sight terrifies me, but not nearly as much as the sounds that came out of the black.

Another stream of ones and zeros pours out of the green-eyed machine man's mouth.

"0100100100100000011011000110111101110110011001
0100100000011110010110111101110101"

I'm in a park. I'm getting married. Dexter is on my left, smiling. We all look beautiful.

I'm in a bar scribbling notes furiously. I can't come up with the right words for her headstone.

I'm in the hospital. She'd dying of cancer. I spoon Jell-O into the delicate slit that was once her mouth.

We're in college. We're going to a movie. Trying to look cool, I ride in the trunk.

I'm walking home, and she's waiting for me. The stink of another woman is on my pants.

I'm in the bedroom. I can hear the hard purr of the beast in the corner followed by the deep rumblings of its hunger. Chains rattle. They're not the firm clinks of a contained animal. They are the serpent-like rustles of a beast loose from its bonds.

Another stream of ones and zeros pours out of the green-eyed machine man's mouth.

"0101100101101111011101010010000001100001011100 1001100101001000000110011001101111011100100110011 011010010111011001100100010101101110"

I'm sneaking into Dexter's house. He's dead, and I'm staring into the bloody eye of his wrist.

It's my birthday. Dexter gives me a gun. My wife uses it to kill herself. The ricochet shatters my life.

I'm in a hospital. Radiation rattles her cancer weary body. "It hurts to breath," she says.

I'm at home, playing games. K.O. I lose. Continue? I feel like I'm bleeding out of a wound that never closes.

I'm at the Hayward Estate. David begins molding my face like it's made out of clay. He screams and I smile because I think I deserve it.

I'm holding her in my arms as she dies. All of her dreams drain out of a smoking bullet hole.

I'm in the bedroom and a digital version of my wife is holding me to the ground. The beast in the corner howls. Its wrath is only an inch-and-a-half of digital wood away. I know it's almost over. I know that I'm the only thing holding it back. I know that I'm the one who put the chains on the door. And I know that the second I let my guard down – the very moment I let go – this beast will be on top of me.

I'm in a room inside a computer, and I'm staring up at the face of my dead wife.

"Who are you, Jack?" she asks.

"I don't understand," I say.

"Game over," She says.

A stream of ones and zeros pours out of the green-eyed machine man's mouth.

"01100111011000010110110101100101001000000110111 1011101100110010101110010"

"Control. Alt. Delete," she says.

"I don't understand." I say. "Am I dead?"

"You already died, Jack," she said. "You're a walking corpse."

"I don't like it."

"I know."

"I never wanted it to be like this."

"I know."

I looked into her eyes. They were beautiful.

"It wasn't my fault," I cried.

"I know."

"I never wanted it to be like this."

"I know."

"I'm sorry," I choke on emotions so heavy they're crushing me.

She cocks her head and smiles.

"I forgive you."

A dozen locks click open and a weighty chain clangs to the floor. A moment later the closet door shatters – splinters spit in all directions. A hearty growl issues from deep inside the darkest part of my closet.

And my beast lunges forth – finally free.

0101000001001100010000010101010001000110010011110101 00
100100110100100000010010100101010 1010
011010101000000100100100100
11100 1000111

CHAPTER TWENTY-FOUR: PLATFORM JUMPING

My watch alarm chattered with life the next morning. For the second time in a week I awoke in a sweat of heavy breathing. I jerked up from Dexter's desk with a groan. The muscles across my neck were wound so tight it felt like needles were trying to push their way into the back of my eyes. I straightened slowly to the sounds of a cracking, sore back. My body hated me. I wasn't too happy with it at the moment. Out of what felt like a whole life of terrible sleep, I might have just endured the worst night ever.

The sun was coming into view; its light spilled over the top of my monitor and warmed my cheeks. I looked down at the screen. On display was the spoiled, hollow city of Shrine – more specifically, the fountain of Galatea. I had no idea what time I had fallen asleep. Nothing I had experienced last night felt like a dream.

I got up and limped to the restrooms. I was surprised to see a sheet and pillow ruffled into the corner of one of the couches we kept near the reception area. It looked like Shinji didn't make it home after all. He hadn't wanted to see Evi again, but he hadn't wanted to be alone either. His compromise was to sleep in the lobby.

Before I entered the bathroom, something else caught my eye. One of the bullpen windows was open. Along the edge of the window's frame I could see the edge of Shinji's shoe. It looked like he was standing on the ledge of the building ready to jump.

I ran.

"Shinji?"

After sticking my head out the window, I could see that he was just sitting on the ledge of the building. He dazedly looked out across the skyline as if he were sitting on the beach. I starred at him for a moment. He seemed oblivious to my presence.

"Just getting some fresh air," he said without looking over.

I crawled out to join him. The ledge was larger than it had looked, and I eased comfortably into a spot only a few feet from him.

"I used to come out here in the mornings when I was the first person in the office," he said.

"It's peaceful. I like it."

Below us a few cars honked, and off in the distance a fire engine blared. A visible layer of pollution was beginning to stream off the streets, but we were above all that. That was part of some other world. Somewhere above us, we could hear the sweet morning songs of nesting birds. When I looked straight ahead, I could see the beauty of an early San Francisco sunrise, gleaming off the glass buildings. The skyline looked like it had been cut from crystal. Behind it all, the ocean flashed a shade of amethyst I'd never seen from it sandy shores. There was a kind of natural harmony to this secret place.

"No one's ever caught you up here?" I asked.

"No."

Shinji continued his lazy stare into the horizon. A few floors down, in the building across the street, I could see a secretary starting her morning schedule, making coffee and sorting letters. I had to wonder if she'd really never noticed Shinji during any of her morning routines.

"Did you find it?" he asked.

"What?"

"Did you find what you needed? Did Evi have any answers for you?"

I surveyed the street below as I mulled over the question.

"I don't know. I feel...different."

I looked over at Shinji. Waited for him to look at me.

"How does it get like this Shinji? How do we ever let it get so bad that our loved ones kill themselves? How can we be so oblivious to a life that's falling apart right in front of us? How many little mistakes does it take to get to that point?"

Shinji didn't answer.

"We bleed to death out of a million little cuts," I said.

"Are you talking about Dexter?" he asked.

"No," I sighed. "I guess I'm not."

"Well, they're still good questions."

I felt my feet grow heavy as they dangled off the edge of the building. Gravity tugged on them and I was too weary to pull back.

"You know," I said. "I never wanted to make mistakes in the first place. I didn't get married with the intention of ruining it."

Shinji grunted.

"Sometimes I feel jaded. I feel like I have to obey rules just because they're rules. But, you know, just the easy ones – like don't drink and drive or pay your taxes on time. We've created a world that tells us what to do and when to do it. We have programs that calculate exactly how much money we can spend every month, automated telephone systems that call and remind us when to see the dentist, lights that show us when it's okay to cross the street."

Staring down at the city below was vertigo inducing, and my feet were feeling very heavy now. I leaned back and let my butt slip a little towards the lip of the building.

"But, I'm always putting that world to the test. I'm always edging towards those lines I can't cross. Because what I really want – what gets me more excited than anything else – is finding out how much I can get away with before getting caught."

I slid another inch towards the edge; an inch closer towards a deadly fall. I was taunting fate…or friction.

"But, I'm also really good at self-deception. I think that as long as I'm above the line I'm okay. It's like I don't understand the danger of living constantly on the edge."

My butt was halfway off the side of the building now. Eight stories had never felt so high. This was it. I could end it right here. It would be so easy. I could just slip off and it would all be over. I wouldn't have to deal with the guilt or the pain anymore. It would only take a second – one tiny moment of weakness.

"Careful you don't sit too close to the edge," Shinji said.

I shifted in my seat so that I was in no danger of falling.

"I walked too close to one of those lines, and it led me into the bed of the wrong woman," I said. "It's a mistake I'll never be able to fix."

Shinji remained silent, but respectfully attentive. I was about to break into tears, and I wiped the moisture from my eyes. I was too proud to let it run down my face.

I quickly changed the subject.

"Shinji, there's something I've wanted to ask you for awhile, but if you don't want to tell me because it's too personal, or whatever, I understand. If I'm crossing the line, just let me know."

"What is it?"

"What did you see in there?" I flicked a thumb back at the computer in the office behind us. "When you were with Evi, what did it say?"

Shinji thought for a bit. He picked up a pebble from the ledge – a piece of chipped stone no bigger than a fingernail – and rolled it between his fingers.

"My grandfather had a saying, 'self pity is an expense too lavish for a noble man.' He used it as a kind of moral to a story he always told. He said that when he was a young man, he was engaged to marry a woman from a neighboring town. She was born of a noble family who happened to be very wealthy. He said he was very fortunate to be in love with such a wonderful woman, and he was excited to start their happy life together."

Shinji tossed the pebble into the air and caught it.

"However, another man also claimed to love this girl. He was a very disturbed person, and he wouldn't accept her spurned advances. He continued to profess his love to her, and as her wedding with my grandfather grew closer this other man became violent. Then, two days before the ceremony, the girl vanished. After a three day search, they found her body in the forest. She was being cradled by the man who'd claimed to love her. Poisons had taken both their lives. My grandfather was crushed; he said a piece of him died that day."

Shinji stopped. I waited for him to finish the story, but it looked like that unsatisfying climax was the end.

"I don't understand," I said.

"Jack, my grandfather died two days after his eighty-fourth birthday. He had lived most of his life in a small town in northern Japan, and he was a stubborn, angry old man. My father said, 'he had become so obsessed with the past, that he forgot how to live.' In all my memories of him, I can only recall one moment where he looked truly happy."

"When was that?"

"It was the moment in that story when he started talking about his lost bride."

I said nothing.

"Evi showed me that I was going to die just like my grandfather. I was going to grow old and alone. I would lie rotting in a house for nearly a week before anyone found my body. And I would be so unpopular that the full assembly of my funeral would be two old co-workers and a local priest."

"I'm sorry," I said, apologizing for nothing.

Shinji was quiet.

"I don't think Evi predicts the future. Hiro said it doesn't control anyone. It just shows you what you need to see."

He nodded, rolled the pebble between his palms one last time, then set it back down on the ledge where he'd found it.

"Do you want to know what Evi showed me?" I asked.

"No."

I smiled. I wouldn't have known where to start anyway.

"Do you think Mr. Hayward will disband ESP?" Shinji asked.

"Yes," I said honestly. Shinji deserved honesty. "Which is fine; it wouldn't be the same without Dexter."

"What are you going to do with Evi?"

"I don't know...Put it in a box. It's not evil. It's just dangerous and misunderstood. I don't think Dexter would want me to kill it."

I smelled the salty morning air. For the first time in a long while it didn't hurt to breathe. My life was full of pain and joy, but I was ready to live and experience them both again. I moved towards the window. There was something I'd been waiting for, for two years.

"Where are you going?" Shinji asked.

"Home. It's time for me to get some sleep."

"But the day just started," Shinji said.

"Yeah," I said, moving back into the office. "But now I feel like I can actually get some rest."

ABOUT THE AUTHOR

Ben Reeves is a writer, journalist, beer maker, and geek sponge. For the last five years he has worked as an editor for *Game Informer Magazine*. He has a passion for video games, comic books, science fiction (or facts), and nearly every other thing that got you picked on in high school. *Kill Screen* is his first novel.

Made in the USA
Charleston, SC
24 July 2012